JET

SUSAN HAYES

ABOUT THE BOOK

Looking for love on all the wrong planets? Try the Star-Crossed Dating Agency.

As the first Pyrosian ambassador to Earth, Jet has his hands – and his schedule, full.

With protesters at the gate, VIPs on the way, and the population of an entire planet to win over, he's got no time for distractions like getting kidnapped.

This book contains an heiress who puts everyone's needs ahead of her own, and a diplomat who has never been in a situation he can't talk his way out of…until now.

SERIES READING ORDER

Star-Crossed Alien Mail Order Brides

Joran

Vader

Kash

Tarjen

Torel

Radek

Karos

Jet

Vykor

SUSAN HAYES

Jet (Book #8 of the Star-crossed Alien Mail Order Brides Series)

First Print book Publication: October 2019

Cover Design: crocodesigns.com

Editor: Dayna Hart

Published by: Black Scroll Publications

ISBN: 978-1-988446-54-7

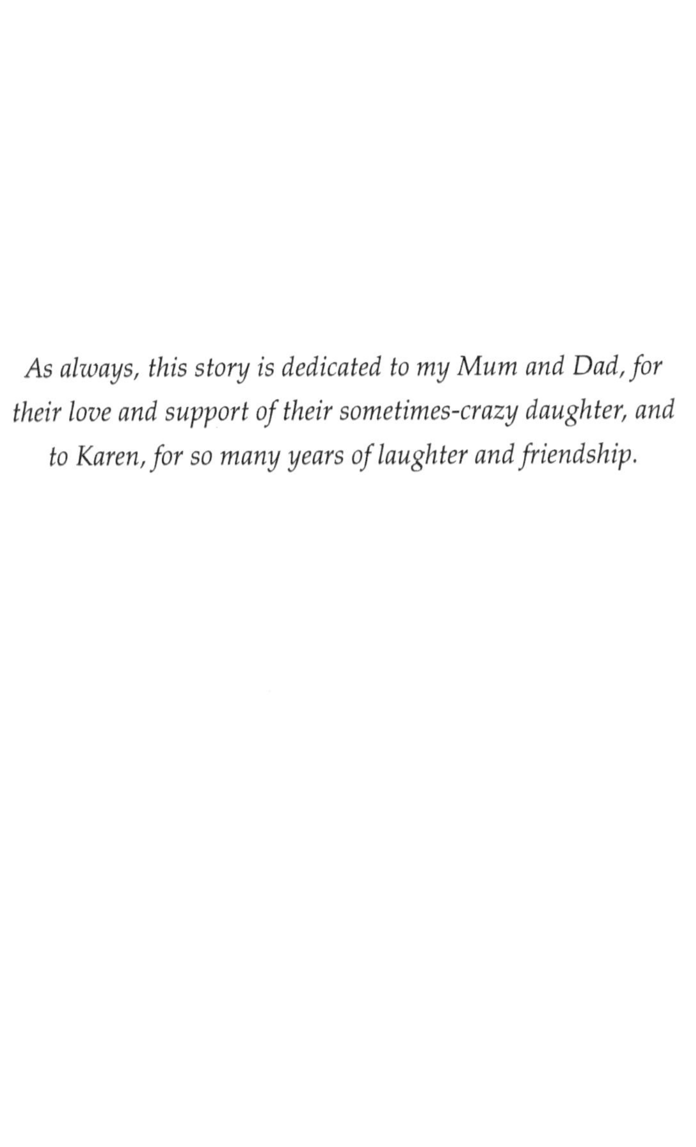

As always, this story is dedicated to my Mum and Dad, for their love and support of their sometimes-crazy daughter, and to Karen, for so many years of laughter and friendship.

CHAPTER ONE

TODAY WAS AN IMPORTANT DAY, and Jet Tindor had done everything in his power to ensure it went as planned. So far, most of his diplomatic assignments had been straightforward. He'd met with various human leaders and representatives of special interest groups, giving them tours of the newly opened embassy and building strong relationships. It was some of the most enjoyable, meaningful work he'd ever done, and he was damned good at it.

Since the bombing of the Gathering at a local sports stadium almost two years ago, keeping open communication had become even more important. His species were here by invitation, and there was always a chance that invitation could be revoked. It wasn't likely, not when Pyros was sponsoring humanity's application to the Inter-planetary Counsel, as well as providing them with advanced technology and knowledge they wouldn't develop for years on their own.

Today's meeting was different, though. The humans he was meeting today weren't motivated by planetary trade or political gain. They wanted what was best for the people they represented, which made his job more challenging. There was too much at stake for this to go sideways, and if things went well, it could change thousands of lives, both here and on Pyros.

He spent most of the limo ride to the airport going over his notes so he'd be prepared for any questions Ms. Dewan might ask. His research led him to the conclusion that Hanna Dewan was an exceptional female. She was bright, focused, and from all reports, a skilled negotiator, whose work took her to some of the most dangerous parts of this still somewhat primitive planet. He wasn't sure if that made her crazy or courageous, but it certainly made her interesting.

She had committed her life to helping women in war zones escape predation and the horrors of the battlefields to start new lives in safety. Today's meeting was an important step in forging a deal that could see many of those human females, and their children, coming to live on Pyros, where females were rare and children of any species would be welcomed.

His companion stirred in the seat across from him, and Jet pulled himself out of his thoughts. "You ready?" he asked Vykor as they turned onto the road that led to the private airfield where they'd meet their guests.

"If I said no, would you let me stay in the limo with Kyle?" Vykor asked, raising one blonde brow in hopeful inquiry.

"Not a chance. You haven't left the embassy in a month. You need this, and I need you."

Vykor shook his head. "I don't see why." He gestured to the elegantly appointed vehicle around them. "This is what you're best at, Jet. Diplomacy and deal-making come naturally to you. I think the future of Pyros is in good hands."

"For someone who doesn't think he has anything to contribute, that was remarkably diplomatic. For a Romaki." The dragon race wasn't known for their tact. When you wielded magic and could transform into a magical creature the size of a small shuttle, you rarely needed to watch what you said.

"I'm a special case, remember?" Vykor smiled, but the expression stopped before it reached his multi-coloured eyes. They marked him as unique among his species. "When you're a freak, words are your best defence against fear." He paused before adding, "Fast-talking is how I avoided getting beaten up more than I did."

Jet nodded and leaned forward, his hands raised, palms up. "And that's why I need you. Ms. Dewan and her people are understandably cautious about this plan. You're good at reading others and putting them at ease."

"I thought this whole thing was the human female's

idea. Why would she be cautious?" Vykor frowned, then answered his own question. "Never mind, I get it. If this happens, she'll be entrusting you with the protection of some of the most vulnerable humans on the planet. Ones who have already suffered too much."

"Exactly." He grinned at the Romaki. "See, this is why I wanted you along. Plus, your English is better than Karos'. Why that male can't use contractions is a mystery only the Gods can explain."

Vykor snorted. "He does it on purpose, to make himself sound more serious. Not as an affectation, but because duty and honour mean everything to him."

Observations like that were why he'd started mentoring Vykor in the art of diplomacy. Not just because he could use the help, though that was part of it. The fact was, the Romaki had the talent and raw ability, all he needed was polish and a little encouragement. Polish was something Jet knew all too well. As the eldest son of the House of Tindor, he'd spent his life in the refined but dangerous world of court politics. His family had been next in line to the throne of Pyros until Prince Joran had claimed his mate, thus securing his claim to the throne. Jet's father had had aspirations of one day ruling the planet.

The day Joran had returned with his lovely human mate, his father had raged at the Gods in a fury, while Jet had sent up a prayer of thanks. Soren Tindor craved power for its own sake, which wouldn't have been good for Pyros. Unlike his father, Jet had never wanted the throne. As far as he was concerned, it came with too many responsibilities and expectations. He far preferred his new role here on Earth. For the first time in his life, he was free to make his own choices, far from the pressures and politics of family and court.

Jet nodded in agreement. "Karos is a serious sort, but knowing he's in charge of security lets me sleep better at night, especially with the Humanity First Movement still trying to cause trouble for us."

Vykor grinned, his expression faintly sardonic. "Since when do you spend your nights sleeping? From what I've heard, you're out almost every evening enjoying everything Earth has to offer."

He didn't deny it. "It's my job to show the humans we're friendly, not fearsome. I can't do that if I never leave the embassy." He raised an eyebrow and looked pointedly at the blond male. "You know you're welcome to join me."

"I know." Vykor ran a hand over his jaw, scratching idly at the freshly trimmed blonde stubble as he considered. "Tell you what. When we're done with this assignment, I'll take a night off and come with you."

"Good. We're about as far from our old lives as we're ever going to get. I don't know about you, but by the flames of the First Ones, I plan on enjoying every second of freedom I can." One day, his parents would find a way to haul him back to Pyros. Until then, he was going to live his life his way, rules and expectations be damned.

JET STOOD beneath the protection of one of the umbrellas their driver, Kyle, had handed to them as they left the limo. The rain had lightened, but each gust of chill winter wind sent a fresh wash of raindrops over them as they waited for their guests.

The door of the craft swung open, and a female stepped out, her heels ringing on the metallic staircase set in place to help them descend. She took a moment to scan the area, her expression intent, turned, and nodded to someone behind her.

"Clear."

Jet recognized the female from the briefing information he'd been given. She was Hanna's bodyguard, Megan Richards, and apparently, she took her job very seriously.

Richards moved down the stairs, and another female appeared at the door. He recognized her from the file as well, but by the Flames of the First Ones, the photo had not done her justice. Hanna Dewan was beautiful. The images had not captured her innate grace, or the intelligence that gleamed in her eyes. Eyes she fixed on him. She then offered him a smile that made him forget about the cold, the rain, and even his carefully rehearsed words of greeting.

He walked out to meet her, shaking out the second umbrella he held and lifting it over her head as she reached the ground. "Welcome to Vancouver, Ms.

Dewan. I'm Jet Tindor. It's a pleasure to finally meet you."

She turned to him, nodded, and dipped into a slight bow. The western custom was to shake hands in greeting, but embassy protocol discouraged casual contact with unmated Pyrosians here on Earth. A single touch between true mates could trigger the Spark, which would be followed by the rapid onset of the Scorching, an undeniable mating fever.

"We've spoken so often I feel like we already know each other, Mr. Tindor."

This close to her, he could see the delicate lines that touched the corners of her eyes, and he noted there were hints of silver in the shoulder-length waves of her black hair, though she was still a woman in her prime. "Since that's the case, perhaps you would consider calling me by my first name?"

The lines around her eyes crinkled slightly as her lips curved into a subtle smile. "If you will call me Hanna."

"It would be my pleasure." He turned and nodded toward Vykor who was greeting the rest of her party. "This is Vykor Halek from Romak."

Vykor offered her a quick smile and a nod. "A pleasure."

"This is my security specialist, Ms. Richards, and my personal assistant, Ms. Ashton." Hanna nodded to the dark-haired female he'd already noted, then to a quiet female with blonde curls who was busy organizing their luggage.

With the introductions done, they all turned and made their way to the limo, though Jet noted with amusement that Vykor was walking with Hanna's assistant, holding an umbrella out for her while he held onto a bright pink carry-on case with his free hand, leaving him exposed to the weather.

Hanna glanced back, her soft lips quirking into a brief smile as she saw what was going on. "Chivalry is not a forgotten art on your planets, I take it?"

"It is not." Jet noted the expression of approval that flashed across her features. "Though there aren't many females on Pyros, those who remain are treated like the treasures they are."

"Treasures tend to be kept in vaults," she pointed out as they arrived at the vehicle.

Jet caught her meaning immediately, but took a moment to think before speaking. Since he'd stepped into this role, he'd spent hours speaking to Princess Maggie and many of the other human females who now lived on Pyros. Their experiences were as different as they were, but they'd all told him the same thing – they valued their freedom above all else. "Not on Pyros. The human females living there made it very clear that they would not be happy locked away. There was a – let's call it a period of adjustment for everyone involved."

Hanna ducked into the limo, but not before he caught the enticing hint of another smile on her soft lips. "I'm sure there was. Will I be allowed to speak with some of the women on Pyros?"

He joined her inside, claiming the seat beside her so they could continue their conversation. "I couldn't stop that from happening, even if I wanted to. Princess Maggie and several of her advisors are all eager to speak to you, and if you decide to visit Pyros, I imagine there will be a great many females who will be happy to talk to you about their lives and experiences on my homeworld."

He leaned in slightly and lowered his voice to a conspirator's whisper. "Especially if you bring along some chocolate. It's still a rarity on my world."

"So, not even Pyros is perfect. Good to know."

The others joined them, the two females sitting across from them, their backs to the driver, while Vykor claimed the seat on the other side of Hanna.

Jet leaned back in his seat and enjoyed a moment of self-indulgent reflection. He'd prepared for this meeting, things were going well, and soon, this agreement would be finalized.

Flames, he loved this job.

Hanna Dewan was used to men trying to charm her. She hadn't expected the Pyrosian diplomat to use the same tactics, though she was willing to admit he was better at it than most. He was poised, well-spoken, and ridiculously good looking. His dark suit was perfectly tailored, as was his jacket, and both did nothing to hide his well-muscled body. He had dark brown hair cut short, and while his jaw was shadowed with stubble, it was perfectly trimmed, giving his otherwise composed appearance a slightly rakish air.

She'd seen the media coverage, of course, but she'd learned long ago not to believe anything she saw on the media. Images, like words, could be manipulated too easily to be trusted. Now she'd met him, though, it was apparent that he was exactly as he appeared in various interviews. No wonder the women of Earth were signing up to the Star-Crossed matchmaking service in droves. If she were ten years younger, she'd be tempted to sign up herself.

Not that good looks and charm were factors for the women she represented. They weren't looking for romance or a fairy tale ending. They just wanted food, shelter, and safety. If the Pyrosians proved trustworthy, then she might be able to give hundreds, maybe even thousands of women a better life.

"Tell me about the ships that travel between our worlds," she asked, moving into information-gathering mode. They had a lot to cover during her visit, and she wanted to hear every detail in person. "How long does it take? How many passengers do they carry?"

"The ships can make the journey in a few weeks, including the time it would take to shuttle the passengers from Earth. The larger ships can carry several hundred passengers at a time and still provide everyone with their own quarters."

"Several hundred? So, if the women shared space, we could fit more?"

"Of course. Though vessels that size are all under the domain of the military, which means that the females would be sharing the common areas with soldiers. I imagine some of these females would find that difficult, considering what they've endured."

His insight impressed her. She'd met dozens of politicians and bureaucrats in her life, and none of them would have considered the women's reaction to a military uniform. Men like that had never been victims. They didn't understand what it was like to have been abused by those who were supposed to protect them. "That's a good point. Perhaps a smaller ship would be better. It would also make things easier to process them when they arrive on your world."

Jet frowned. "Process? In what way?"

"Documentation. Surely they'll need some? Not to mention time in quarantine, maybe even temporary housing until they can arrange for sponsorship?"

Jet's eyes narrowed, then widened in understanding. "Ah. Our process would be quite different than what you're used to. There will be no quarantine. Each female will go through a brief, painless decontamination process as they debark the shuttles onto the main ship. They'll receive an ident chip and other necessary items before they arrive on

Pyros, and permanent housing will already be arranged for each of them. The princess felt that it would be best that each group be settled in the same area, so they can support each other through the transition period, though of course they will be free to settle anywhere they'd like. The human females living on Pyros have already organized job training, and of course, each female would be provided with cognitive augmentation so they are fluent in the various dialects of my species, as well as cultural information and everything they would need to flourish there."

Hanna blinked, too shocked to speak for several seconds. She'd known the Pyrosians were eager to have more human females on Pyros, but all their conversations so far had been focused on establishing a rapport and ensuring that both sides were trustworthy. "They'll have housing? Training? No camps? No quarantine?"

Jet waved a manicured hand. "By the time they arrive, each and every female and her offspring will be a citizen of Pyros already. They will be welcomed."

"But there would be no requirement for them to accept a Pyrosian mate, correct?" They'd already discussed this detail, but now they were face to face, she wanted to hear him say the words, even if it meant risking insulting him.

Instead of taking umbrage, Jet smiled, rising several more places in her esteem, and the tiniest flutter of butterflies erupted in her tummy. Oh no. She was not developing a crush on the dashing diplomat. This was work, not play, and besides, he was at least a decade younger than she was. This was no time to turn into a cougar.

"Any female who wishes to do so can add their names to the mating database at any time after they arrive, but per our agreement, it would not be required."

She hadn't planned on asking this question yet, but the timing was too perfect. "Why is that?"

This time, his smile made her breath catch. He wasn't *that* good looking.

"You're asking me what we get out of this deal?" the modern-day term rolled off his tongue, accompanied by a roguish smile.

"I am."

"Children. The women, and their children will be citizens of Pyros. Even if they don't grow up and take Pyrosian partners, they'll still play important roles in the future of my species. Our population is dwindling, leaving holes in our workforce and in every other facet of daily life on my world. And if some of those children return to Earth, then they will bring with them a wealth of information, along with what we can hope is a positive opinion of Pyrosians."

"Future diplomats?" she asked, amazed at the scope of his answer.

"They will be the future, period. For both of our species."

The answer was diplomatic, but she sensed he was sincere. Beneath the grand words were real hope, and hope was her stock in trade.

She took a moment to compose her thoughts before she spoke again.

Megan was staring out the window, no doubt looking for threats. It was what she was paid to do, but Hanna trusted the Pyrosians to keep them safe. Megan hadn't been happy to hand over security to the aliens, but it was a necessary sign of trust, even if her bodyguard didn't approve. She caught Megan's eye and gave her a hint of a smile, along with a subtle hand sign to confirm that things were going well. Megan raised a hand, and then all her attention shifted to the window again.

"Hold on!" Megan shouted, and Hanna had a split second to grab hold of her seatbelt before the world around her erupted into chaos. The vehicle shook, metal screeched, and she was flung against her seatbelt as they spun wildly. As the vehicle finally came to a halt, rocking on its tires, stunned silence fell, though she could barely tell over the hammering of her heart.

"Everyone okay?" Megan's voice broke the silence. Her tone was sharp, but her eyes were too wide, her normally ruddy skin too pale. "I'm alright. What happened?" Hanna asked as the others confirmed they were still in one piece.

Megan ignored her question and started issuing orders, instructing Lily to call the authorities then directing Jet to contact the embassy, all while undoing her seatbelt. "I think we were rammed intentionally. I'm going outside to take a look. Everyone else stays here, and lock the door after I'm gone. Vykor, if anything happens, can you transform and get the others out of here?"

Vykor didn't get a chance to answer before the driver's partition lowered behind Megan.

"Kyle, you okay up there?" Jet called to the driver.

"Did the other vehicle drive off?" Megan asked.

A man's hand appeared in the gap above the partition. He shoved something through and then the partition closed again. Before any of them could react, a series of heavy clicks sounded. She knew the sound. Someone had activated the door locks. They were trapped.

Jet was still unbuckling his seatbelt when Megan grabbed the canister that had been dropped into their section. It started to hiss and vapour spilled out of one end.

Gas. The word flashed through her mind even as she pulled loose one end of her scarf and used it to cover her face.

"Everyone cover your mouth and nose," Megan instructed, her voice confident and full of command despite the insanity of the situation. Everyone around her was trying the doors, but the gas was rapidly filling the vehicle and it was getting hard to see.

Megan pivoted in her seat and started kicking at the

window, but Hanna knew it wasn't going to work. The vehicle was armoured, the windows designed to withstand gunfire. She knew, because Jet had told her about it to reassure her that they were taking her safety seriously.

Apparently, they'd missed something. The thought humoured her, and dark, desperate laughter bubbled up inside her. She clamped her lips tight and tried to think of something she could do, but it was getting difficult to think at all. Her eyes watered, her lungs burned, and her vision was going dark.

She wanted to scream. To fight. To do something, but her limbs were too heavy, and her eyes were closed tight against the stinging, suffocating gas. She sagged, leaning into Vykor, but it was Jet's voice she heard. "No matter what happens, I will protect you."

Then the darkness rose around her, and she couldn't hear anything anymore.

CHAPTER TWO

JET WOKE UP, and for a moment wondered what he'd done the night before to earn the mother of all hangovers. His mouth was parched, his eyes seemed to be glued shut, and his bed was moving so much it was making him queasy. It took him a moment to register that he couldn't be in bed. Whatever he was lying on was hard, flat, and vibrating slightly. He could also hear the low thrum of an engine, along with the distinctive sound of traffic moving over rain-slick roads. *Shit.*

He forced his eyes open, but it didn't help. His vision was obscured by dark fabric. Turning his head brought on a wave of dizziness, but it also made it clear he was wearing a bag over his head instead of a blindfold. He flexed his arms, or at least he tried to. They were bound in front of him, his wrists and elbows lashed together so tightly he could barely move them.

His legs were immobilized, too. What the hell had happened? He fought through the disorientation and dizziness, trying to remember. He'd been at the airfield. Met with Hanna. They'd been driving. They'd been rammed. Gassed. Kyle had betrayed them.

Where were the others? Were they okay?

The vehicle jarred and bounced as they drove over something, and he heard a female's low, pained groan from somewhere to his left. He turned toward the sound. "Hanna?"

Something heavy pushed him onto his back, slamming him to the hard metal floor. Whatever it was pressed down on his chest and making it almost impossible to breathe. "No talking, ya alien asshole." Someone spoke from above him. Jet guessed the weight on his chest to be the other male's boot.

"Chill out. Boss left orders not to damage this one, or the women," another male said, his voice harsh.

The pressure eased and he sucked in a lungful of air, grateful to know that Hanna and the other females were unharmed, at least for now.

"What about the other one?"

"The dragon? Boss didn't say anything about him. We were only supposed to be bringing back three of them."

Three? Coils of icy dread wrapped around his spine. There were five of them in the vehicle, not including that traitorous *sarkeen,* Kyle. If he and Vykor were here, which one of the females had been left behind, and why?

"Dragon?" The weight on his back vanished as the first male took two shuffling steps back. "Why the fuck is it here? Those things are dangerous!"

"Jesus, nut up already. He's no threat. He's some kind of mutant. Can't shapeshift or whatever the fuck they do. No magic, either. And the Pyrosian isn't mated. No mate means no fire. So, find your fucking backbone and do your job."

"I'm doing it. But they're aliens, man. No telling what weird shit they're capable of."

The other male snorted in derision. "You're pathetic. Did you sleep through the briefings? We know exactly what they're capable of. Jesus, did you even read the handouts?"

Jet listened to the two males talk and tried to gather as much information as he could. Whoever had taken them were organized and well informed. Had Kyle been the only inside source, or were there others? How had they slipped through the regiment of interviews and background checks? Karos would be losing his mind by now. The big Romaki would take this attack as a personal failure.

Karos, Keth, and the others back at the embassy must have found the vehicle by now. They'd already be searching, and Gods have mercy on these fools when Karos found them, because the fire dragon certainly wouldn't.

"Where are you taking us?" Hanna asked, her tone as calm as if she were asking the time. She was an amazing female.

"I said no talking!" There was a thump and a faint hiss of pain.

"Dammit, Mike. I fucking told you not to hurt the women! Get your ass over to the door and stay there. Bossman is going to break you in half when he hears about this."

"Stupid bitch shouldn't be hanging around with these alien assholes," Mike muttered, but he was already moving farther away, his voice and shuffling tread growing fainter.

"Hanna, are you hurt?" Jet asked softly.

"Stop fucking talking," the words were heavy with warning, but Jet didn't care. Bullies were the same, no matter what planet they were from. They only responded to one thing, strength.

"Not until I know the females are alright."

The male growled but didn't say anything.

"Hanna?" Jet asked again.

"I'm okay."

"Me too. Oh, and it's Lily talking." She paused, then called out, "Vykor?"

"For fuck's sake, you're all fine, but you won't be if you don't shut the hell up. This is a hostage taking, not a play date."

Jet wanted to know if Vykor was alright, but he

couldn't risk it. The one in charge had stated that only the females and Jet were to remain unharmed. Given the way these males were acting, they were likely to take out any frustrations on Vykor. At least he knew which of the females was missing. Megan Richards, Hanna's bodyguard.

He offered up a silent prayer to the Gods that no harm had come to her. When he'd taken this job, he'd been eager for the responsibility, for the chance to do something meaningful. Now, the full weight of that responsibility settled on his shoulders. He'd offered these females his protection. Now, two of them had been taken, and one's fate was unknown. He clenched his fists and tested the bonds that held him. The plastic ties bit into his flesh until he bled, but the pain gave him focus and clarity. He'd need both.

HANNA LAY STILL and did her best to ignore her aching ribs. The brute who had kicked her might not have used his full strength, but it hadn't been a love tap, either. She was hurt, scared, and disoriented. All valid feelings, but none of them were helpful, so she pushed them aside.

She was grateful to Jet for asking how they all were, despite knowing it would come at a cost. Hearing their voices, even for a second, helped ease her worries and reminded her that she wasn't alone. It also gave her new reasons to fear. Megan wasn't with them.

There's no way she could have escaped, which meant their attackers had left her behind on purpose.

She hoped it was because abducting someone with Megan's skill set wasn't a good idea. But if they'd figured that out, they might have also decided that leaving her alive wasn't in their best interests, either. Her heart twisted at the thought of what might have happened to her friend, but Megan had drilled into her head, time and again, that if something like this ever happened, she was not to worry about others. Her job was to stay alive.

"I'll be coming after you. Your job is to stay in one piece long enough for me to find you," Megan's voice sounded in her head, the memory providing a small bit of comfort. Megan was the toughest woman she'd ever met. Hanna had to believe she was alive and royally pissed off. Whoever had taken them, they were going to regret it.

It wasn't long before the truck came to a stop, the squeal of worn brakes announcing their arrival and setting her teeth on edge. There were footsteps, grunts, and then a wash of cold air flowed over her as the doors were opened. Even through the hood there was no mistaking the scent of the sea—salt and seaweed, mingled with the smell of diesel fuel and rusted metal. Seagulls called to each other from somewhere nearby.

"Free their legs and get 'em on their feet," The one in charge ordered, and within seconds rough hands were cutting through the plastic ties on her legs. There were groans and muffled sighs of relief as everyone was cut free and helped out of the truck.

A hard hand clamped onto her shoulder and she was guided inside. It was warmer in here, but not much. The cries of the gulls faded away, replaced by men's voices that echoed as if they were in a large space.

"Put the blonde in her cell, and bring Dewan and the diplomat to me," a new voice ordered, this one full of arrogance rather than authority.

"What about the other alien asshole?" she thought it was Mike who asked, but she couldn't be sure.

There was silence for several seconds before the arrogant one snarled in frustration. "Fuck. Put it with the blonde, but secure it to a chair or something."

"You're putting it in with one of our women?" a new voice demanded. *How many of these jerks were there?*

"You questioning my orders now?" The tension in the air thickened, and Hanna wished she could see. There was too much going on.

"No boss. Just clarifying. I mean, we're supposed to be protecting our women from these freaks, right?"

"Right. But you're going to secure the creature, and it's not like we have anywhere else to put it. I'm running a revolution, not a fucking hotel service."

Someone, she'd given up trying to tell the voices apart, barked another order. "You and you, escort the prisoners to their cell. I'm going to go get something to secure the creature."

There was a rush of activity, people moving, and she wished she could at least see Lily once before they were separated. At least the girl wouldn't be alone. They were putting Vykor with her, which meant they'd be able to watch out for each other.

"Bring the others to my office. I want to speak to them."

She was shoved forward hard enough she staggered a few steps, and the leader from the truck growled. "Stop manhandling her. We need her and the diplomat in one piece, remember?"

"If you could please take this hood off, then I wouldn't be so likely to trip." She hated to ask these jerks for anything, but making demands wasn't going to accomplish anything, and she really wanted the damned hood off.

They walked a few more feet, then the floor changed from concrete to carpet and the temperature rose to almost pleasant levels.

The arrogant voice spoke again. "Polite, meek, and sensible. Very well. Danny, you can take Ms. Dewan's hood off."

"Yessir."

The hood was removed, and she blinked until her eyes adjusted to the bright lights that filled the room.

Eventually she was able to make out a few objects: a battered old desk, a few plastic patio chairs, and a rickety card table with a printer and a few office supplies sitting on it. An ancient space heater sat beneath the table, the filaments glowing cherry red. *It's a wonder the whole operation hadn't burned to the ground already.*

She rubbed her bound hands across her face, using the motion to check for the necklace she always wore. It was gone. *Damn.*

The necklace had been a gift from Megan, and she never took it off. Along with the sentimental value, the pendant held a tracking device. If it was missing, then either their abductors had scanned her for such devices, or someone had told them about her necklace. Only a few people knew about it. Megan, of course, her parents, so they wouldn't worry so much about her, and Lily. Lily had a tracker of her own, though hers was part of a charm bracelet. Had they found hers, too? How had they known about them at all?

She put that line of thinking on hold and focused on the here and now. There would be time to consider things later, and maybe by then she'd have more information to work with. Standing behind the battered desk was a man with dishwater blond hair and a broad, bulky frame. He was dressed in a flannel shirt, and what she could see of his jeans were stained and well worn. He looked more like a down-on-his-luck handyman than a terrorist. The only thing about him that stood out were his eyes, which were a rare shade of blue so deep they almost looked purple. She knew someone else with eyes that colour, and her instincts started whispering that it wasn't a coincidence. She just couldn't make the connections, yet.

The man was watching her intently. "Better?"

She breathed a sigh of relief at having the hood gone, pasted a smile on her face, and said, "Much better, thank you." The gratitude galled her, but Megan had taught her that in this scenario it was better to be cooperative.

"You're welcome. I wanted to speak with you briefly and let you know what's going to happen." He pointed to one of the plastic chairs. "You may sit, Ms. Dewan."

"You have my name, may I have yours?" she asked. As she took a seat, she noticed there was one more occupant in the room. A dog the size of a small pony lay in the far corner of the room in a nest of shoddy blankets. She didn't know much about dogs, but this one looked like it was one-part Rottweiler and two parts hellhound. It didn't move, but the animal's dark eyes were alert, watching herself and the others with intent interest.

"My name is John Ashton, and I'm the current leader of the Humanity First movement."

It all came together in an instant. Those eyes. That name. She knew this man. Well, she knew *of* him, and she barely managed to hide her shock beneath an impassive mask. Their captor was Lily's half-brother.

The poor girl would be devastated when she found out her family was involved.

Unless she already knows…

Hanna dismissed the thought the moment it appeared. There was no way Lily would be part of anything so vile as the Humanity First movement. They represented everything Hanna and her team were fighting against.

"I'd say it's nice to meet you, but, well, given the circumstances…" she raised her hands to gesture around them and then lapsed into silence.

"Mr. Ashton, may I speak?" Jet interjected.

She glanced over at Jet. He was still standing, flanked on either side by two men wearing the same style of clothing as their leader, and they both looked shabby compared to the Pyrosian. Even bound and hooded, Jet projected an aura of quiet confidence that she would have found attractive if their situation wasn't so freaking dire.

He was standing at something like parade rest, though his arms were in the wrong position, and his voice was steady and firm. She was impressed. Either he was fearless, or he was a better actor than she would ever be.

"No, you may not. The humans are talking right now." Ashton turned his attention back to her, his expression predatory. "Where were we?"

"You were going to tell me what happens now," she prompted, trying to keep her voice soft.

"Indeed. It's simple enough. I want two prisoners released, and I'm willing to trade the two of you for them. As we speak, arrangements are being made to contact your people and start the process."

"But there are four hostages," Jet spoke before she could.

"You were not given permission to speak." John nodded to his men, and one of them cuffed Jet across the face. "I need you in one piece, but I won't let that stop me from correcting your manners while you're here."

To his credit, Jet took the blow without flinching or uttering a sound, but she knew it had to hurt. She spoke up, hoping to distract their captors from Jet. "Please, Mr. Ashton. Lily is just my personal assistant. She has no value as a hostage, and releasing her might go a long way to proving your intentions."

"I'm not releasing anyone. Your assistant has already proven her worth, and the second alien might prove useful. The two of you are too valuable to risk injuring, but the other one...well, if the authorities balk at my demands, I'll have a hostage I can use to demonstrate my *intentions*."

Her stomach curdled. These were fanatics driven by fear and hate. They wouldn't hesitate to hurt or even kill Vykor if they thought it would advance their cause. She didn't know what to make of his comment about Lily. Was he deliberately trying to sow distrust?

Lily wasn't in contact with anyone from her family

apart from her mother. Her brother was an asshole, just like their father had been.

Ashton hummed in satisfaction as another thought occurred to him. "The other alien will also do nicely as a whipping boy. If either of you cause problems, he'll pay the price. Do you both understand?"

"I understand," she and Jet replied at the same time.

"Good. My men are going to escort you to your cell now. Do not speak to anyone. Don't make trouble. If everything goes to plan, you'll only be my guests until tomorrow."

It wasn't long before Jet was pushed through a doorway of some kind. Rough hands pulled off the hood, and he stumbled forward a few steps, barely stopping himself before he smacked into a metal wall. The only light came from the door he'd come through, but he could see well enough to watch as Hanna walked through another door to his left. It took his scrambled senses a few seconds to notice the bars between them.

"A shipping container?" Hanna queried as she looked around. "This is where you're holding us?"

"It's not so bad. You got a bed, a toilet, and privacy. Hold out your hands." A big, rough-looking male stepped into view. He was holding a blade, and when Hanna tentatively held out her hands, he cut away the plastic straps that bound her arms and wrists.

"What privacy?" she asked, gesturing around the small space. Each cell was less than three meters wide and maybe three meters across, small enough he could cross the length of his cell in three long strides.

"We put up a curtain, so the alien freak can't stare at you while you're sleeping or nothing." The male nodded to a lightweight length of fabric hanging by the bars of Hanna's cell. It could be run along a piece of string to divide their cells, but neither the string nor the fabric was sturdy enough to do anything with.

"Shut up, you idiot. We're not supposed to talk to them," another male appeared at the door to his cell, his face screwed up with the effort of trying to pull the heavily barred door across the doorway. Like everything else in the cell, the door appeared to be hastily put together, and it stuck in its track. He was tempted to give the male a hand just to be contrary, but he resisted the urge. Anything he did to upset these males might be taken out on Vykor. He couldn't risk it, so instead he watched the male struggle with the cell door in silence.

This male was young, with a patchy beard and acne, and the gun belt he wore was too big for him. It was canted over one hip, the combined weight of the gun and holster slowly dragging the male's pants down to his ankles. Where were they recruiting, the local education centers?

"Just telling the lady she doesn't have to be gawked at." The male on Hanna's side retorted.

"Thank you." Hanna flashed the male a smile.

"Welcome." He actually blushed as he retreated from the cell, clearly overwhelmed by that small amount of female attention.

"Hold out your hands." The lanky youth said to Jet. He was holding a boxcutter and gestured for Jet to move closer. He put his hands through the bars, wincing as the youth hacked through the plastic straps binding him. Jet held his breath and stayed perfectly still until it was done. He already had a lingering headache, bruised ribs, and another bruise forming on his jaw—he didn't need to add more injuries to the list.

By the time his bonds were gone, Hanna's cell door was shut and their guards moved on. He took a quick glance through the bars of his door and caught sight of the two males standing guard about ten meters away. They stood facing each other, level with what Jet estimated were the ends of their converted container. It gave them an overlapping view of the cell area and made sure there were no blind spots around them. What it didn't allow them was a direct view of their prisoners. Maybe he could take advantage of that.

"How's your jaw?" Hanna asked, her voice soft but steady.

"Just bruised." He stepped back from the door in time to see her tap a disk on the wall. It immediately started to glow. He found one on his side and activated it. Together, they cast enough light to illuminate their surroundings, such as they were.

"Ugh. Guess the budget didn't allow for indoor plumbing." Hanna wrinkled her nose in distaste and gestured to the back corner of her cell.

There was a small, beige, boxy object sitting there. It took him a few seconds to recognize what it was. A primitive toilet. He had one in his cell, too. There was a roll of toilet paper and a packet of hand wipes on the floor beside it. The only other furniture they had was a metal bunk that appeared to be welded to the back wall. There was a thin mattress set atop it, along with an equally thin-looking blanket.

"You're amazing," he told her, and he meant it. He'd known trained soldiers who wouldn't be as calm as she was right now.

She gave him a startled look. "What? Why? All I've managed to do today was get taken hostage. Believe me, you're not seeing me at my best."

He walked over to the bars that separated them and leaned up against them. "Why? Because we've been kidnapped and tossed in a cell, and you're cracking jokes about our captors' budget. Because you went face to face with the leader of a terrorist group and never showed a second's weakness. You're incredible."

She laughed, though there wasn't much humour in her voice. "Sadly, this is not my first time being kidnapped."

It was unfathomable to him that the males of this

world could put their females at risk the way they did. His species was on the brink of extinction because there weren't enough females, and there were parts of this planet where females were treated as lesser beings with no rights and no value. Even the males who had taken them hostage were treating her as if she were nothing more than a bargaining chip.

And it was his fault she was here.

"I'm sorry this happened. We failed to protect you and your people." He turned to face her, fingers gripping the bars that separated them. "I will do everything I can to protect you from whatever happens next."

"This doesn't all fall on your shoulders." She walked to him, her eyes solemn and sad. "Your driver might be with these men, but John Ashton has a connection to someone in my camp, too. I'm certain he's related to Lily, which means that somehow, my assistant is involved, though I have to believe she's involved unwittingly. We both have a share of the blame. We'll just have to find our way out of this together." She brushed her fingers over his, and a brilliant blue spark arced between them, making both of them jump.

She stared at her hand and then looked up at him with a look of utter disbelief that matched what he was feeling.

"Was that what I think it was?" she asked, her words barely a whisper.

"I...uh. I think so." The Spark. A sign from the Gods

themselves that they were mates. It couldn't be, but…it had to be. Hanna was his true mate. Flames, what were the Gods thinking?

"Here? Now? You?" Hanna's shock mirrored his own.

He reached through the bars to take her hand. "Here. Now. Us."

CHAPTER THREE

MATED? Oh, no, no, no. This couldn't be happening. Hanna stared at Jet and then dropped her gaze to their joined hands. *Shit.*

"How?" she blurted out with all the awkwardness of a teenage girl trying to talk to her first crush.

Jet shrugged and tightened his grip on her hand. "Blame the Gods. It's what I'm going to do."

"I don't believe in any gods." After the things she'd seen, the cruelty and suffering she'd witnessed, she'd lost faith. If there was a higher power, how could they allow these atrocities to happen to innocent people?

"It would appear the Gods of my world have interfered in your life, whether you believe in them or not. You are my true mate, Hanna Dewan. Which makes me a very fortunate male."

She tugged her hand out from under his and stepped back from the bars. "You call this fortunate?

We're prisoners." Her voice cracked a little, and she paused, forcing herself to lower her voice before she attracted the attention of the guards outside. The last thing she wanted was for one of them to overhear that she might be mated to an alien. Which she couldn't be.

Could she?

Jet turned to face her, his blue eyes fixed on her face. "We're prisoners, yes. And that's the only reason I found you. If we were at the embassy right now, we'd be making polite small talk and working on a way to bring your dream to fruition. We'd never have this moment. We would have never touched, and never initiated the Spark."

His words moved her, but they didn't change the facts. They were in danger, locked away from the world and each other. They couldn't do anything about the Spark even if they wanted to, and she wasn't sure he truly wanted this. He'd been raised to accept that the Spark meant he'd found his mate, and that was supposed to be a great thing, but she couldn't be what he wanted. She was older than he was. She couldn't have kids. The only part of her that hadn't started to sag or soften was her mind. "I'm not sure finding each other was a good thing."

Jet gripped the bars that separated them tight enough his fingers whitened. "Why would you say that?"

"You want a list? For starters, we're not even in the same cell. If this is really happening, then the only way to ease the effects of the Scorching is if" —she blushed and gestured to him and then her—"we get together. Tough to do when there are steel bars between us. No *togetherness* means the Scorching is going to make it next to impossible for us to think clearly, and we're only going to survive this mess by being smart. Then there's the whole *us* thing. You're an attractive young male, and I'm a middle-aged woman. I can't possibly be what you want."

"You find me attractive." He grinned and loosened his hold on the bars. "That's a good start."

She almost laughed. "Out of everything I just said, that's your takeaway? Really?"

"I heard every word you said, my *tani*. And you're right about almost everything. The bars, our situation, the danger. But you're wrong about one very important thing." He reached through the bars, hand out, palm up. "I was impressed by your intelligence and commitment before we ever met. You are lovely, determined, and brave. Why wouldn't I want you?"

Her thoughts scattered like dust motes in sunshine. He thought she was lovely? Most men only thought that until she started speaking. Then they'd describe her differently. Intense. Single-minded. Driven. Stubborn. Cold. And those men were the same age as her. Jet was... "How old are you?"

"In Earth years? Thirty-five or so."

She'd guessed right. There was a decade between them. "You're too young for me."

He smiled again and damned if it didn't make her traitorous heart beat a little faster. "Apparently, the Gods think otherwise."

"Your Gods are insane, and if you're good with this. then I've got some doubts as to your mental state, too."

He chuckled, then wriggled his fingers in a come-closer gesture. "I'm more than good with this. You are my *tani*, my treasure, and I will protect you with my dying breath."

She took his hand before she knew what she was doing, and he drew her back to him with a slow, steady pull. Her heart pounded, and her thoughts raced in an incoherent whirl so unlike her usual careful, deliberate calm. It was unsettling, and at the same time, intoxicating.

"You should be with someone your own age. Your own species. My work is here, I'm not leaving Earth. I can't." she was babbling now, trying to make him see why this wasn't right. Why they couldn't happen, though the closer she got to him, the harder it was to remember all the reasons it wasn't a good idea.

He grimaced slightly. "I came to Earth to get away from my family and the entire planet. I have no intention of going back there if I can help it. My life is here now. Why would I return?"

"Because that's what your species does. Take women from my world and move them to yours. That's the whole point, isn't it?"

"Finding mates for my people is my purpose.

Finding you…" He drew her in close to the bars, pressing his face between them to steal a gentle kiss from her. "Finding you was a surprise. I'm here to help both our species find their way toward our shared goals. Perhaps the Gods think I needed someone to help me do that. Someone like you."

As his lips touched hers, she gave herself a second's reprieve from reality. One brief, glorious moment where she could pretend that this handsome, charming man was actually hers. "Maybe."

He knew Hanna didn't really believe they were mates. Not yet. He was still trying to come to grips with that fact himself, and he was Pyrosian. The Spark and what it heralded had been part of his life since childhood. He just never expected to experience it. There were no mates for him on Pyros, and he'd been too busy trying to make a place for himself on Earth to even consider looking for one here. And yet, here she was. His mate.

This changed everything. His work here might be focused on bringing prospective mates and children to his homeworld, but he'd never wanted children of his own. It was one of the reasons he was here, where his parents couldn't harp at him day after day about his duty to find a mate and procreate. The last thing he wanted was to create more lives for his father to manipulate. Would Hanna want children? As an ambassador, would he be allowed to get away without having them now he had a mate? Would the Gods betray him that way? He hoped not.

He let go of Hanna's hand and reached for her, wrapping an arm around her waist and pulling her closer. The bars were in his way, but he ignored them, needing to feel her soft body against his. Her scent filled his lungs, and the sweet taste of her lips exploded on his tongue, branding his senses. He drank her in, committing every detail to memory. This was the female the Gods had chosen for him, and while he might question their timing, he couldn't question their choice. She was perfect, and she was *his*.

The Scorching flared to life as he kissed her, a rush of heat and need that had him hard in seconds. Flames, he wanted her. He had no idea how to make that happen, though. Not, yet, anyway.

It took a few seconds for his lust-addled brain to notice that Hanna had stopped kissing him, and a few more before he managed to summon enough will to lift his head and look down at her.

"We need to stop," she said.

"Probably, but that doesn't mean I want to." Looking into her amber eyes was like being bathed in sunlight, warm and welcoming, tempting him to kiss her again.

"Let go of me." She took a half-step to the side, putting enough distance between them to let him think a little more clearly.

He released her waist but kept hold of her hand. He wasn't ready to let go of her entirely. He wasn't sure he could. *By the flames of the First Ones, this shouldn't be happening so fast.* It had to be the Scorching messing with his thinking, but it had only been a few minutes since they'd touched.

Hanna glanced down at their still-joined hands pointedly, but she didn't pull free. Was she feeling it, too?

"Why are you still holding onto me after I asked you to let go?" she asked, her tone more amused than upset.

"For the same reason you haven't let go of me. You must feel it, the pull between us?"

Her brow crinkled in thought, then she nodded. "I feel something. It's like I'm a little drunk. It's hard to focus on anything but you." She blushed a little. "Please tell me this is the Scorching thing, and I haven't turned into a twittering teenage girl again. Anything but that."

He chuckled, admiring her strength yet again. This couldn't be easy for her, but she was still cracking jokes. "I've got good news. You're still a gorgeous, very grown up woman."

Her lips twitched into a ghost of a smile. "Temporary insanity, then. I can deal with that."

He lifted her hand to his mouth and brushed a delicate kiss across her knuckles. "I suspect you're more than capable of dealing with anything the universe can throw at you." He winced and glanced up at the ceiling. "But to be clear, that was not an invitation. We've got enough to handle for the moment."

Hanna laughed, a soft, breathy sound that made his cock throb. "We really do." She lowered her voice to a bare whisper. "Any thoughts on how we're going to get out of here?"

"Not yet, but—" He was cut off by a woman's shriek.

"You bastard! I would never help you do something like this!"

"You tell him, Lily," Hanna murmured in an approving tone.

There was a sharp crack, and a soft cry that was almost immediately drowned out by a male roar of fury. "Don't you touch her!"

Jet cursed through gritted teeth.

Hanna paled, gripping his fingers hard as they listened in horrified silence. Lily cursed and pleaded, her words punctuated by random sounds of violence.

By the time the outburst ended, Hanna was shaking. He thought it was with fear, but when she spoke, he realized she wasn't afraid, she was livid.

"That arrogant bastard. He did that on purpose. He's hurting them to remind us he's in control." Her voice was thick with rage, and her amber eyes gleamed.

He shared her fury. "I know. And he's going to pay for it. We're walking out of here, *tani*. All four of us. I'm not accepting any other outcome."

"I believe you." She sounded a bit surprised by her declaration.

"I meant it."

"I know you did. Your eyes…they flashed bright gold as you said it. Is that a thing with your species?"

"They did?" If he needed further proof that the Scorching had hit him, that was it. Gold eyes meant he was mated.

"They turned gold. Just for a second. Is that something I should be worried about?"

"No. It just means that the Scorching is coming on quickly. It varies from pairing to pairing. Strong emotions will trigger a temporary change. After we are mated, the gold colouring will be permanent. At least, that's what I was told."

"We're not mated, yet." She moved away from him again, and this time it was even harder to let her go, but he did it. Convincing her they belonged together was just another kind of negotiation, and he knew better than to rush the process any more than it already was.

"No. But if you feel what I am, you know it's only a matter of time."

She tapped a perfectly manicured fingernail against one of the bars separating them. "I don't see how that's going to happen. Besides, I think we have more important things to focus on right now."

He could almost see the walls she was erecting between them, and he was having none of it. She was his mate, damn it. Unlike some of his brethren, he knew better than to fight the Gods' will. From what he'd heard, it never went well, and it didn't change anything, anyway. They were destined for each other, and he wasn't going to let something as minor as steel bars or a kidnapping get in the way of destiny.

HANNA EXPECTED Jet to crack a joke or make some glib remark, but he didn't say anything. The silence hung between them, giving her a chance to take another look at him. A real look, one not filtered by her preconceived notions or expectations. It was a skill her father had taught her as a child. She'd been born into wealth, which meant learning young how to judge other people's character, to get a sense of who they really were, and what they might want from her.

There was no denying he was handsome. It had been one of the first things she'd noticed when she looked him up as part of her research into the Pyrosians. His smile could be classified as a weapon of mass seduction, and he was the poster boy for everything a woman could want in an off-world Romeo. Wealthy, well-spoken, and attractive. She acknowledged that this was her perception of him and then looked past it. Who was he, really? What did she know about him?

The man in front of her was fit, with a hard, muscular frame beneath his perfectly tailored suit.

Between that, the predatory, alert way he moved, and the stance he'd taken in John's office, she realized he must have been in the military. She'd seen enough soldiers to recognize one, even out of uniform.

He was protective of her. Had been even before the Spark. He had courage, too. And she knew from their emails and phone conversations that he was astute, quick-witted, and he seemed sincere in his wish to help bring her plans to fruition.

So, was she shutting him down because it was the smart thing to do, or because it was easier to come up with excuses than to accept that this insanity was actually happening?

He shifted, leaning one shoulder against the bars as he watched her, watching him. "What's going on inside your head right now?" he finally asked, breaking the silence.

"I'm trying to figure out which one of us is crazier."

"Any preliminary thoughts you want to share?" He lifted both brows and gave her another dazzling smile that made it hard to think.

"When you smile at me like that, most of my thinking stops."

He cocked his head. "Maybe that's the right response. I've read the reports about what happens to males of my species who go into denial. It's emotionally and physically messy, and they end up mated anyway. Which is why I'm not going to fight this. So, you see, I'm not crazy. I'm actually being quite logical. Which means..." He lifted a dark brow and grinned.

"Did you just imply that I'm the crazy one here?" She managed to keep herself from laughing, but only barely. Somehow, Jet seemed to know exactly what to say to make her laugh, even when she shouldn't. He was too damned charming for his own good, and definitely too charming for her sanity.

"I only pointed out that I'm applying logic to our situation, *tani*."

Her entire body quivered when he uttered that last word. There was something about the way it rolled off his tongue, or maybe it was the look in his eyes when he said it. "What does *tani* mean? You've called me that several times, now."

"Roughly translated, it means treasure. And that is what you are. A rare and priceless gift." He shrugged out of his suit jacket and passed it through the bars. "And right now, my treasure is cold. You're shivering. Take my jacket."

She wasn't about to admit that her shiver had nothing to do with the chilly cell and everything to do with him, so she took the jacket and wrapped it around her shoulders. It was still warm from his body heat, and she snuggled into it, burying her hands in the fabric with a contented sigh.

"I am not jealous of a piece of clothing. I. Am. Not," he grumbled, his eyes heating again as he watched her.

She ignored his comment, though she couldn't hide

the way her cheeks heated. "Thank you. I didn't realize how cold it was in here." She looked over to her bed and the sparse bedding provided. "It's going to be a long, cold night."

"Even longer if they don't feed us." He straightened and strolled over to the barred door of his cell before calling out in a remarkably humble tone, "I know I'm not supposed to talk to you, and I promise to be sorry about it later, but is there any chance of getting a meal for the human females?"

She tensed, expecting the guards to react in anger, but instead one of them called back. "Food for the ladies, yes. Food for you, no. We're not wasting food on no alien assholes."

She hurried over to her doorway, pasted a grateful expression on her face, and looked outside. "Thank you so much. I'm starving."

"Dinner's coming soon." The same big guard who had spoken to her earlier raised his hand in a brief wave, dropping it again before he was seen.

"And now we know they'll be coming by with food eventually. With any luck, Vykor or Lily heard us, too, so they'll know we're okay." Jet moved away from the door, shrugged, and sat so his back was to the outer wall, out of sight of the door. "We also know the big guy likes you, which might be useful."

"And neither of them seemed bothered by the fact you talked to them. It was a big risk for you to take, though. What if they'd gotten angry and taken it out on

Vykor? He's Romaki, but he's not like the others, is he? If he was, he'd have done something to fight back by now."

"Vykor is the only Romaki to ever be born without a dragon's spirit." Jet patted the floor on her side of the bars. "Sit. I know the floor is cold, but if we use the bunks, we risk being overheard, and we need to make plans."

Overheard. The word sent her thoughts racing. "Damn. What if they have cameras? It might not be safe to talk at all." She started patrolling the room, scanning every crack and crevice for recording devices. Not that she had much of a clue what to look for, but she needed to do something productive, and this *felt* useful.

Jet got to his feet and did the same, which made her feel better about her sudden attack of paranoia. It might be pointless, but once they'd looked, she could stop worrying about cameras and focus on the hundred or so other critical matters left to deal with.

"I don't see anything suspicious. This whole setup is pretty basic. No place to hide a camera," Jet said.

"I think you're right." Their captors had clearly put the cell together quickly and on a shoestring budget. She'd already seen how clunky and awkward the installed doors were to use, and a cursory inspection of her sleeping area revealed that the bunk's edges were jagged, sharp enough to cut, with messy, unprofessional welds holding the whole thing in place. She eyed the bunk's welds again, then looked at the bars dividing their space. She didn't dare say anything in case she jinxed it, but she crossed to the bars and crouched to take a close look at the point it met the floor.

"Found something?" Jet asked, crouching on the other side of the bars.

She pointed to the weld holding the bar in place. Even she could see it was too thin to hold properly, and there was a visible crack across the join. "Bad welding job. The bunks are the same."

"Do you think it's weak enough we could work one of these free?" He gave the weld an almost idle kick, and the crack widened. Not much, but enough she could see the change.

"Is it the same at the top?" she asked.

He rose onto his toes to check the ceiling. "I think so. Flames, this could work."

They examined the rest of the bars, looking for the weakest one. Maybe there was something to Jet's belief in the Gods because the weakest of the bunch was the one closest to the door, which meant no one could see it unless they came inside the cell.

"Those welds might be weak, but it's still going to take some work to break them. We're going to need some kind of leverage." Jet looked around and sighed. "The blankets might work, but they could tear in the process. We need something heavier."

"What if I asked my guard for more blankets? He might give me something we can use."

"Good thinking." Jet gave her an approving smile

and reclaimed his former position on the floor, back to the wall and his long legs stretched out along the bars. "Join me? We still have things to talk about."

She went to her bunk and snagged the lightweight blanket off it, and wrapped it around her shoulders before settling down beside him on the cold, hard floor. She was tempted to kick off her shoes, too, but for the moment she kept them on. Heels weren't comfortable, but neither was having cold feet. "What do you want to talk about?"

"A few things. For one, you managed to get them to take off the hood, so you saw a lot more than I did. I need you to tell me what you can remember about the layout, the number of people around, and anything else you can think of." He reached through the bars and set his hand down on her thigh. "Then, I want to know about you."

"I imagine you've already read all about me. Everything there is to know is online somewhere." At least, everything she wanted to be known was there.

He patted her thigh. "I don't mean where you were born or how much your shares in your family's mining company are worth. I mean, I want to know about *you*. What's your favourite food? Your least favourite? What kind of books do you read? Flames, you're my mate. I want to know everything about you."

She freed her hand from the blankets and laid her hand over his. It wasn't the smartest move, but she couldn't seem to help herself. She needed to touch him. "I'd rather hear about you."

He chuckled. "Nice deflection. Does that usually work?"

"Honestly? Yes. Most people would prefer to talk about themselves. Especially the kind of people I deal with most of the time. Why doesn't it work on you?"

He turned his hand over and interlocked their fingers. "You're forgetting something."

"What's that?"

He gave her a slow, sensuous smile that turned her brain to jelly. "I'm not people. I'm Pyrosian." He leaned in and pitched his voice to a low murmur. "And I am your mate."

Her heart thundered against her ribs and her breath caught in her throat. As she watched, his eyes flashed gold again, and she leaned in closer to the bars. "I'm starting to believe that. And it scares the hell out of me."

CHAPTER FOUR

THE SCORCHING WAS INTERFERING with his ability to think, but there was no missing the truth in Hanna's words. "So, being kidnapped you can joke about, but being mated to me has you scared?" He raised a hand to his chest. "I think my ego just took a fatal blow."

She uttered an amused snort and rolled her eyes. "I doubt it's fatal. Your ego seems quite healthy. I've seen you on enough television interviews to know."

"That's not the real me, though." He decided to answer her honesty with some of his own. "I got this post, in part, because I can step into that role and make it work."

"If that's not who you are, then you're a good actor. I believed it."

"I grew up in the royal court of Pyros. I had what you humans call a good game-face by the time I was six years old. Projecting confidence and authority, even when you have no idea what you're doing, is a required skill in my family."

"Your father is, or was, in line for the throne, wasn't he?"

"He was. Now that Prince Joran is mated with a child of his own, it is unlikely a member of my family will ever sit on the throne." He didn't bother keeping the relief out of his voice.

"You don't sound unhappy about that."

"Unhappy? Flames no, I'm thrilled. I spent my entire life being prepared for a role I never wanted. I like Joran. I respect his father. And I knew better than anyone how bad it would be for Pyros if my father ever became king. As far as I'm concerned, this is the best outcome for everyone."

Her eyes widened. "You didn't want to be king someday?"

"Never. That kind of responsibility carries so much weight. Every decision the king makes affects the lives of an entire planet. Everyone pays attention to the smallest details, looking for clues or leverage. It's an exhausting way to live, and I'm happy to be free of it. The day we learned Joran was mated, I went out and celebrated. I didn't come home for three days."

"And how did you end up here? Earth is a long way from the court of Pyros."

"Exactly." He grinned. "I visited Joran last year and asked him for a favour – I wanted to be sent to Earth.

It's as far away from my parents and their expectations as I could get."

She laughed. "And I thought my family was difficult. I never needed to flee light-years to get away from them. Halfway around the world seems to do it."

"You, too? Given the work you do, I would have thought your family would be nothing but supportive."

"My work is too dangerous for their liking. Too many visits to war zones, not enough time trying to meet a nice man to settle down with. They've given up on getting grandchildren from me, I'm too old, but they're still hoping for marriage and a nice quiet homelife."

"I don't see you being the type to stay home and organize charity events while someone else goes to the front lines. You'd never be happy like that." He didn't have to know her well to recognize she wasn't the kind to let others take the lead. If her parents couldn't understand that, then they didn't know their daughter any better than his parents knew him.

"Congratulations, you already know more about me than my ex-husband."

He already knew she'd been married. Her past was exactly that, the past. It was her future he wanted to be part of.

"Why did your marriage end? I know it didn't last very long. You were divorced before you finished your law degree."

She gave him a sidelong look. "Clearly you read more than just my website biography."

"You came to us with a plan that could alter the fate of my species—of course I researched you. I needed to know what kind of person you were, and if you could really deliver what you were suggesting."

"Then why are we talking? You know everything about me already." She tugged at her hand, trying to free it, but he tightened his grip and didn't let her pull away.

"We're talking because reading about someone isn't the same as *knowing* someone. I want to know you, Hanna. So, tell me why it ended, because I can promise you what we have is not going to end. Not until the day we take our last breath."

"You can't be sure of that. Surely some matings fail? It can't be a perfect match every time."

"You're deflecting again."

She shot him an irritated look, and he bit back a laugh. Teasing her was fun.

"Fine. My marriage failed because we wanted different things. We both wanted to change the world, but I thought we'd do it together. He wanted to do it alone, while I stayed home to play housewife and mother. He knew I didn't want a family, but he thought I'd change my mind…" she shrugged. "I didn't."

"Then your former husband didn't know you at all. As for Pyrosian pairings…it's different than with your species. A true mating never fails. That doesn't mean things are always perfect. Couples on Pyros fight. They argue, hurt each other's feelings, and drive each other crazy sometimes." He was talking, but part of his mind was replaying her words. She didn't want a family, either? Could he have his mate and not worry about children?

"But they stay together no matter what?" She wrinkled her nose. "That sounds like my idea of Hell."

"Remember, my species doesn't fall in love the same way yours does. We don't fall out of love, either. The bond between mates is ever-present, creating an intimacy that is missing from human pairings. After you and I are fully mated, that bond will start to grow between us. It might be weak or strong, but even the weakest bond will allow you to feel what I feel at times. You'd know if I were lying, or angry, or in pain. We will be linked for life. I'll know if my words hurt you, or if you are angry or sad. If the bond is strong, then you'll be able to know what I'm thinking."

She gave him a dubious look. "That seems like a sure-fire way to start a fight, not end one."

"At times, yes. But it also means that no matter what, we'll be connected. If I hurt you, I'll feel it." He touched his chest. "Just as you will always be able to feel how much I care for you."

Hanna lapsed into silence. After a moment, she started chewing on her lower lip thoughtfully, and it took every bit of his willpower not to pull her close enough to kiss.

"You've gone quiet," he said after a while.

"I was thinking about what you said and imagining what an effect that would have on the way human relationships worked. So many of the women I rescue have been abused by the men in their lives. If the men could feel what they were doing to their women... it would change everything."

"I can't offer you a way to make that happen here on Earth, but any female who found her mate on Pyros would have that bond. They would never feel a moment of fear around their mate because they'd know they were treasured." He smiled. "Plus, mating a Pyrosian may unlock all sorts of talents. We've had human females become telepathic, empathic, and more than a few who can now summon and wield fire as easily as their Pyrosian mates."

"I'd forgotten about that. In fact, I'm finding it difficult to remember anything right now. I can't focus on anything for long, not even the fact that one of my friends is being held hostage, and another might be dead." She bowed her head and pressed the heel of her hand to her brow. "I hate this."

"It's the Scorching. I don't like it either. This is supposed to be a time of joy and celebration as we get to know each other and allow ourselves to succumb to the mating fever. Instead, we're prisoners, unable to help our friends, or ourselves."

"If..." Hanna cleared her throat and started again.

"If we gave in to this madness, you'd be able to summon fire, right?"

"I would."

She raised her gaze to his, her expression similar to that of a soldier preparing to go into battle. "Then we have to mate. I'm tired of being helpless. If mating you means gaining a weapon, then we need to do it."

It wasn't what he wanted her to say. He'd teased her about being logical about their situation, but now she was doing exactly that, it didn't feel right. He wanted her to want *him*, not see their mating as a means to an end.

"You don't have to…" He didn't finish the sentence. He couldn't, because they both knew better. The Spark proved that they were mates, and the Scorching would not stop until he'd claimed her and completed their mating. Instead of lying to her, he sighed in frustration. "I'm sorry, *tani*. I know this can't be easy for you."

She gave him a lopsided smile. "I'm the one who should be apologizing. I'm pretty sure you're getting the raw end of this deal."

He rose to his knees and turned to face her through the bars. He couldn't do anything about the timing, or their situation, but by the Flames of the First Ones, he would find a way to convince her that he was happy she was his mate. "I don't believe that at all. I think the Gods chose the perfect female for me."

HANNA WASN'T sure if it was the sight of Jet on his knees in front of her or the mind-fogging effects of the Scorching, but she believed him. He wasn't unhappy about their situation. As unbelievable as it was, he actually wanted this. Despite their differences: the gap in their ages, the fact they weren't even the same species. None of that concerned him at all. A flood of desire washed over her, drowning the last of her doubts. Then it hit her, she was lusting after a young man. She was officially a cougar.

She started to laugh and had to cover her mouth with both hands to muffle the sound.

"Care to share the joke?" Jet asked when she finally had herself back under control.

His tone was light, but his eyes were narrowed and his jaw was set in a tight line.

"This. All of it." She waved her hands around the cell, then reached through the bars to take his hands in hers. "Despite everything that's going on, you really want me as your mate. It just made it clear to me that you're the crazy one. You're crazy, and I'm a cougar."

His lips quirked into a shadow of a smile and his stance relaxed. "I believe the human expression is that I'm crazy *about* you. And yes, I know that's the Scorching talking, but that doesn't make it any less real. I want you, Hanna Dewan. That isn't going to change, no matter what the circumstances… including the fact you suddenly think you're a large, predatory feline."

He cocked his head to one side. "Should I be worried about that?"

"No. Well, maybe, but not for the reason you think. A cougar is slang for an older woman who dates younger men." She burst into another round of giggles, burying her face into the blanket as she used the laughter as an outlet for some of her stress. At some point, Jet reached through the bars to wrap his arms around her, offering her silent comfort.

It took a few minutes to get herself together again, and when she looked up, Jet was watching her with a look of pure male contentment. She couldn't remember the last time a man had looked at her that way.

That's because it's never happened before.

"Better?" Jet asked.

She felt foolish, but surprisingly she felt better, too. "Yes, thank you. I think I needed a temporary lapse of sanity to cope with everything."

"I was enjoying the moment, too. It gave me a reason to hold you." He drew her closer, then slanted his lips over hers in a kiss so hot it could have melted the bars between them.

She started to pull away, but she didn't have the strength to resist him. Not anymore. She craved his touch, his taste, the warmth of his body wrapped around hers. She reached for him, running her fingers through his hair and framing his face with her other hand.

He whispered her name and kissed her again,

deeper this time, his tongue slipping into her mouth to dance with hers. The need burning inside her exploded into an inferno and she tore at his shirt and tie, loosening it with clumsy tugs, sending buttons flying as she finally reached bare skin.

"Soon," he whispered, the word rich with promise and a need as deep as her own. "Flames, I have to have you soon, or I'm going to lose what's left of my mind."

"I'm not sure I have much of mine left, either. If I did, I'd be reminding myself of all the reasons this isn't going to work instead of kissing you."

Jet's blue eyes flashed gold again. "This *is* going to work. Trust me, the sooner you accept this is happening, the easier it will be."

"Are you always this cocky?"

He flashed her a boyish grin that reminded her yet again of the difference in their ages. "Only when I know I'm right. I'm the planetary expert on human–Pyrosian relations, remember?"

"It had slipped my mind." Which was true of almost every important thing she should be thinking of right now. One look at Jet and it all vanished in a cloud of glittering lust dust.

"If you don't trust me, then trust in the Gods. They have a plan for us."

"I'm really not good at trusting anyone else to plan my life. Just ask Megan." She sighed as a wave of worry and guilt hit. She'd forgotten about her friend. Again. "Do you think she's okay? If they hurt her…"

"I've been thinking about her. This group is supposed to be fighting to protect human females from alien abduction. If they hurt Megan, they'd lose their credibility."

She thought about that for a second, and the knot in her chest loosened a little. "That makes sense. And if they left her alive, then she'll be coming for us." She absently raised her hand to her throat, reaching for the necklace that had been taken from her.

"She won't be alone. Karos will tear this city apart until he finds us. The Romaki are the fiercest warriors in the galaxy, and they don't stop until their enemies are destroyed."

"It would be a lot easier to find us if I still had my pendant. Megan gave it to me years ago, and it contains a tracking device. They knew about it, somehow."

"They knew a great many things they shouldn't, including the fact we were meeting you today. Kyle is clearly working for them, which worries me. How many others did we miss? This group is far better organized than we suspected, especially given that most of their leaders are currently incarcerated."

She lowered her voice to a barely-there whisper. "Ashton, their new leader, is a dangerous man. I'm almost certain he's Lily's half brother. Same father, different mothers. Their father was an abusive, controlling bastard who died badly. John killed him. Murdered him in cold blood. I don't know all the details, but Lily told me enough to know he's bad news.

John planned the whole murder out carefully, and the only reason he got caught was Lily. She came home from school early and found their father's body before John had time to dispose of it. She called the police, not realizing it was John who had killed him. John blames her for the years he spent in prison, even though it was his own actions that put him there."

Jet was quiet for a moment, then nodded grimly. "You think this is about revenge."

"I think so, at least partially. He's a nasty piece of work, just like his father. At least, that's what Lily says. She won't have anything to do with him. He scares her almost as much as their father did."

"Unlikely she's helping him, then. That still leaves the question of how he knew about your tracker. If she didn't tell him, who did?"

Hanna shook her head. "I don't know. If she's involved in this mess, it was inadvertently. She's one of the kindest souls I've ever met. She's dedicated her life to my Haven Network, working to rescue women from situations like the one she and her mother were in. She'd never help John or anyone like him." She paused. "I just wish I could see her. Speak to her. Megan gave her a tracker, too. I don't know if they took hers. If they didn't, then maybe help is on its way already."

"Help will come. Tracker or not, they'll find us eventually. We just need to be ready when they do."

She knew what that meant. They needed to have sex soon. Sex meant Jet would be able to throw fire. It would be a major advantage, and right now they'd need every advantage they could get. "You'll be ready. We'll make sure of that. Then after this is over, we'll talk about what this whole mating thing means, and how it's going to work."

He cupped her cheek in one large hand, and she leaned into his touch without thinking. *Live in the moment for once. It has to happen either way, you might as well enjoy it.*

Jet must have known what she was thinking somehow, because he moved in closer, his eyes locked on hers. "We will work, *tani*. You and I will be together from now until we return to the Flame that birthed us."

He might have been birthed in Flame, but she'd been born in a hospital in Toronto, right here on Earth. She couldn't see how this was going to work, but for the moment, it didn't matter. They'd talk later. She'd successfully negotiated with despots, warlords, and lunatics. She could manage one charming diplomat, even if he was from another planet.

The more they talked, the more Jet wanted to know about his new mate. Even with the effects of the Scorching tearing at her defences, she was still guarded. He recognized her behaviour. The subtle deflections, the questions she answered with another question or simply left unanswered. Life at court had taught him the same tricks, the same need to be wary.

He wanted to know who had taught *her* those lessons. More than that, he wanted to fix her hurts and show her that she could trust him. It was totally irrational, considering they were almost strangers, but the moment the Scorching had started, reason had gone out the airlock, and it had taken common sense, patience, and most of his sense of self preservation with it.

Their moment of idyllic peace ended in a mad scramble when they heard footsteps coming their way. He got to his feet and started pacing, hands in his pockets, head down, a picture of unmotivated misery.

Hanna wrapped the thin blanket tighter around her shoulders and plonked down on the edge of her bunk with her back to Jet. She hunched her shoulders and hid her face until her guard appeared at the cell door.

"Brought you some dinner." The big male passed a tray through a horizontal slit in the bars near the floor.

"Thank you so much." She raised her head and gave the guard a grateful smile so big it made Jet want to strangle him. She shouldn't be looking at any other male like that. Ever. She was his, dammit. He bit back a snarl and jammed his hands deeper into his pockets.

"I hate to be a bother, but do you think you could bring me another blanket?" Hanna lifted the corner of the one wrapped around her. "This one isn't going to do much to keep me warm tonight."

The guard nodded. "Should be some in the storage room. They should have given you more than just the one. It gets cold in here after dark."

"You stay here at night, too?" she managed to sound completely innocent as she probed for information.

"Right now, yeah. Big things are happening. Boss wants us all here." The guard jerked his head toward Jet. "In case these assholes cause trouble. Why are you with them, anyway? You seem nice."

Hanna's head snapped up. "I'm not with *them*. I was meeting with the Pyrosians to discuss a business deal. The other woman is my personal assistant. She was just doing her job, and now she's locked up with a stranger. An alien stranger. She's okay, isn't she?"

The guard scuffed a boot on the ground, hesitating a few seconds before answering. "She yelled at the boss. I think they know each other. He didn't like that, but she'll be okay."

Hanna breathed a deep sigh of relief. "Good. She's getting food too, right?"

"Yeah."

"Thanks." She retrieved the tray but didn't back away from the door. "My name's Hanna. What's yours?"

He looked around, confirming there was no one else around before whispering, "I'm Chris. I'm going to be off-shift soon, though. If that alien asshole gives you any trouble, you call for Jack, and he'll make sure you're safe."

"Thank you, Chris. That's nice of you. You have a good night."

"Uh, yeah. Me and some of the guys are going to watch a movie, maybe play some cards. I'll see you tomorrow. My shift starts at seven."

"I don't have any way to tell time. How many hours from now is that?"

Chris frowned, then glanced at his watch. "Uh, it's almost seven at night now. So, I'll be back in, uh, twelve hours."

Jet couldn't believe how much information the big male was giving them. No wonder they weren't supposed to be talking to the prisoners.

"You work long shifts," Hanna said sympathetically.

He nodded. "We got to. Not that many of us left to cover things." He winced. "I probably shouldn't have said that."

She laughed. "Who am I going to tell?"

Chris grinned. "True. Okay. I got to go and get you that blanket. Be back soon."

Once he was gone, Hanna carried the tray over to her bunk and sat down, setting the food beside her.

"That was impressive," he said, wandering closer to the bars, his voice pitched for her ears alone.

"I had a good teacher. It's all about making connections, making them see you as a person instead of a prisoner."

"And it helps that you were nice to him," he didn't bother hiding his annoyance over that fact.

"It did help. I've met a lot of men like him. Women too, for that matter. They've been told that everything wrong with their lives is someone else's fault, and they've convinced themselves it's true. Because of that, Chris believes that everything he's doing, right or wrong, is justified because it's for the greater good." She shrugged and sorted through the items on her tray, opening packets and checking labels as she spoke. "People like that expect people to try and change their minds. They almost need it to remind themselves of all the reasons why they're right. If you're nice to them, they're surprised and often end up being nice back."

"In case I haven't mentioned this yet, you're as smart as you are beautiful."

She shook her head and didn't look up, but he could see she was smiling. "And you are the biggest flirt I've ever met."

"I'm not flirting. I'm stating a fact."

Before she could reply, they heard footsteps again, the same heavy cadence as before. Chris was returning, hopefully with the blankets she requested. And once he was gone, the two of them would be alone, likely for the rest of the night.

It was time to show Hanna that he meant every word he'd said. She was his, and nothing in the galaxy could make him regret that fact.

CHAPTER FIVE

TrUE to HIS worD, Chris brought her several blankets, all of them worn but clean. She thanked him, and then lingered at the door to watch him leave as another pair of guards took his place. The night watch had apparently begun.

"Three blankets. He outdid himself. Maybe I'll tell Karos not to eat him when that damned dragon finally shows up," Jet said.

She tossed the blankets onto the end of her bunk, blinking in surprise when something slipped from between them. "He brought dessert." She held up the candy bar Chris had smuggled her. "Chocolate. Decent chocolate, too. If that doesn't earn him a reprieve, nothing will." They had both adopted low speaking voices that wouldn't carry to the guards outside.

"There's a difference? I thought chocolate was just chocolate."

Hanna stared at Jet in disbelief. "How long have you been here? Hasn't anyone told you about the hierarchy of chocolate, yet?" She held up the Dairy Milk bar. "This is acceptable. Not top of the line, but not bad. Purdy's is better. Rogers Chocolate is better still, and European chocolate is better than just about anything made in North America."

"What about Hershey's? I've tried that."

She wrinkled her nose in dismay. "That's bargain-basement chocolate. It's one step above carob, but only barely. When we get out of here, we're going to have to work on your understanding of all things cocoa. This mating thing isn't going to work out if you don't learn to appreciate chocolate. It just won't."

"If that's what it takes to keep you, I'm willing to expand my horizons."

"Your sacrifice is noted." Despite everything, the banter and flirting made her smile and wrapped her heart in a warm, fuzzy feeling that only got stronger the longer they were together. It should worry her, but somehow, it didn't. In fact, nothing worried her for long. It had to be the Scorching messing with her head, and a few other spots on her body.

Shaking off another wave of lust, she gathered up two of the blankets and the tray and carried them to their meeting spot by the bars. She handed one of the blankets to him, laid hers on the floor, and settled into the middle of it with the tray on her lap.

"Thank you," Jet set his blanket out the same way

she had and joined her on the floor, his long legs stretching out along his side of the bars.

She divvied up the food as evenly as she could, handing him one of the bottles of water, then splitting the peanut butter sandwich and passing it through the bars like they were having the strangest picnic on the planet. The fruit cup and lukewarm cup of instant ramen were harder to split, but they took turns passing them back and forth, stealing lingering touches every time. There was only one plastic spoon on the tray, making the simple act of sharing a meal into something far more intimate than she could have imagined.

They talked as they ate, mostly about the layout of the warehouse, how many men she'd seen around, their most likely location in the city, and their chances of being rescued before morning.

"If they had our location, they'd have come for us already. There's no way Megan would wait."

"Karos wouldn't either. He'll show up the second he knows where we are, tear this place apart, and then apologize for letting us get kidnapped."

"Megan might actually start apologizing before she's finished shooting people. She has to be losing her mind right now. I should have listened to her. She told me not to let your people handle security. I didn't listen, and now she might be..." She couldn't finish the thought. Megan had to be okay. She needed to make this up to both of them. Lily and Megan were her employees, her friends, and she'd put them at risk.

Jet reached over and took her hand. "They're going to find us, Hanna. Neither of our friends is the kind to give up. We can't either."

His words settled her a little, and a few deep breaths helped ground her even more. Well, as grounded as she could be given the steady of stream of X-rated thoughts that filled her head every time they touched. "Thank you. I needed the reminder. Megan would kick my ass if she knew I was wasting time and energy worrying when there's work to do."

"Given the day we've had, I'd say we're both entitled to a few minutes of worry." Jet raised her hand to his lips, brushing a few tender kisses to her fingertips. "You taste like peanut butter. I think that's officially my favourite food now."

"That's because we haven't had dessert, yet." She brought out the chocolate bar and offered it to him.

"I think we should save that for later. It's going to be a long night, and we're not going to be fed again until morning." He kissed her hand again. "Besides, I've already got dessert right here."

"How can you go from being sensible to silly in a matter of seconds?" She tugged her hand out of his grasp.

Just then, the lights outside the cell started going out, a bank at a time.

"Stay here." Jet was on his feet in a heartbeat and moved to look out the door of his cell.

"What's going on?" When the lights started going

out, she had hoped it was the start of a rescue, but the silence made her doubt that's what was happening.

"Nothing." Jet sounded as disappointed as she felt. "The guards haven't moved, and there are still lights on in some of the offices. They're probably just trying to save on their power bill."

"Lucky us, we got kidnapped by the low-budget bad guys." She got to her feet, kicked off her shoes, and gathered them up with the remains of their meal. She set the tray by the cell door, placed her shoes beneath her bunk, and shut off the tap-light on her side. Her heels would make too much noise on the steel floor, and she didn't want to do anything to draw attention to what they were about to do.

"Smart thinking." Jet murmured when she slipped back over to the bars. "But your feet must be freezing."

"When we get out of here, I'm taking a long, hot bath and staying there until I forget what it's like to be cold."

"That sounds fantastic. If I bring chocolate, may I join you? I promise to get the good stuff."

She had every intention of saying no, but that wasn't what came out of her mouth. "You, me, chocolate, and a bubble bath? You've got yourself a date."

He winked. "Until then, I will do my best to keep you warm, *tani*. Just as soon as I deal with these damned bars."

He deftly twisted the blanket into a makeshift rope and secured it to the bar they hoped to pull out. It took a few minutes of experimenting, a couple of whispered suggestions, and another few seconds to wrap one of the original, thinner blankets around the bar in hopes it might dampen any sound should it hit another bar or the floor before they could stop it. Any loud noise would bring the guards over to investigate, and that would be the end of their plan.

Jet planted his feet and wrapped the end of the blanket rope around his hands, then looked upward. "If anyone out there is feeling generous, it would be appreciated."

Hanna took a step backward and crossed her fingers. "If this works, I'll have to rethink my stance on the existence of higher beings."

"You are my true mate, chosen by the Gods themselves. Until you believe that, I'll just have to keep the faith for both of us." With that, Jet gripped the blanket in both hands and pulled.

She held her breath, half expecting the blanket to tear or the knots to give. Jet strained, grunted, and then the bar gave way to the pressure with a faint crack as the welding seal snapped.

"It worked!" she whispered in gleeful amazement.

"I told you. It's destiny." He retied the knots at the top of the bar and repeated the performance, only this time she had a job of her own. She sat on the floor and held the base of the bar as tight as she could so it didn't go flying once the top broke free.

At least, that was the plan. In reality, the bar gave

way with enough force it flew out of her hands and smacked her in the chin.

"Hanna!" Jet set the newly freed bar aside and tried to squeeze through the gap they'd made, but he couldn't get through.

"You're too big." The words came out a little muzzy as she tried to work her aching jaw.

"Flames. How bad is it? Are you bleeding?" Frustrated, he dropped to his knees and reached for her. Still dazed, she managed to catch hold of his hand.

"I think I'm going to need you to kiss it better."

"If that's what you need me to do." He drew her into the gap and kissed her, and just like that she forgot about the pain and the dizziness. All that mattered was him.

ONE SECOND she was on her side of the bars, the next, his gorgeous mate was in his arms, her soft body pressed against his. That was all it took to hurl him into the middle of a firestorm that incinerated the last of his patience. He had to have her. Now.

The only thing that stopped him from tearing off her clothes was the knowledge she had nothing else to wear. As much as he wanted her naked, he couldn't bear the thought of another male seeing her that way. "Clothes," he almost growled the word between kisses.

"We're wearing too many," she replied as she started unbuttoning his shirt with shaking fingers.

"Permission?" he couldn't seem to speak more than a single word at a time, which wasn't surprising, given most of the blood in his body was currently in his aching cock.

Hanna moved back so she could see his face. Her amber eyes were bright with desire, her cheeks flushed, her lips swollen by his kisses. "You have it. I'm not fighting this anymore. I can't."

"Me either." They kissed again, though it was more than a simple kiss. It was a prelude, a promise of what came next. He savoured the taste of her, the sweetness of her lips, the warmth of her breath, the way she shivered with pleasure as he explored her body.

They undressed each other quickly, craving skin to skin contact, both of them spurred on by the effects of the Scorching. Flames, she was beautiful. Long legs, golden skin, and soft curves that fit his hands perfectly.

He paused in his exploration long enough to remove his shirt, nearly strangling himself on his tie when he forgot he was wearing it. She laughed, the sound wrapping around him like a silken caress. Gods, he loved her laughter. It was a balm to his soul, a comfort he hadn't even known he'd craved until now.

He sucked her lower lip into his mouth as his hands slid up her flanks to cup her breasts. Her nipples, already hard, pebbled beneath his palms and he shifted his hands so he could tease the taut points with his fingers.

She moaned into his mouth, her hips rolling as she rubbed against him, arching herself into his touch. Somehow, she got her skirt off without losing contact with him, and he changed positions so he was leaning against the wall of their cell, his legs extended so Hanna could straddle them. She reached between them, undoing his belt, and then his pants. When her fingers wrapped around his length he bucked against her hand, nearly unseating her in his urgency. Nothing he'd read, nothing he'd imagined could compare to the pleasure he felt at her touch.

She fisted his cock, stroking it with a firm touch that made his balls tighten and his heart pound. "If you don't stop, I'm going to come before I'm even inside you. That's not how I want my first time to end."

She froze and looked up, stunned. "Your first time. You mean your first time with me, right?" Then her eyes widened. "Oh my god. I forgot. You can't. I mean, you only ever come with your mate. So you've never…"

"Never."

Doubt dimmed the light in her eyes as her body went tight with sudden tension and she let go of him, pulling her arms in close to her sides. "I'm worse than a cougar. I'm a freaking cradle robber."

First cats, now cradles. There were definitely some gaps in the cognitive augmentation program because he had no idea what she was talking about. "Why would you steal a child's bed, and what does that have to do with my lack of experience?"

"Because you're a virgin, and I'm… not even close to that. I shouldn't want this. What will people say when they find out I pulled a Mrs. Robinson?"

Again with the strange references, but Jet was starting to grasp the problem. He ignored her stiff-backed resistance, pulled her in close, bowed his head over hers and murmured, "I'm a grown male, Hanna. I've never had sex before, but I'm hardly an innocent or a child. I've been a soldier, which means I've seen hardship and death. Enough of it to know when a good thing comes along, only a fool would walk away. You're a good thing, Hanna Dewan. The best thing that's ever happened to me."

"Those are lovely words, but will you still mean them when this Scorching thing is over? If we stop now, then maybe…"

"There's no stopping this. You know that." He stroked her hair as he spoke, trying to soothe her worries, but it wasn't easy, not when his control was shredded and his need for her was making it hard to think.

"You're so sure of yourself. Of this. What if you're wrong?"

"I'm not wrong." He coaxed her head back so he could look into her eyes. "Trust me, *tani*."

She shivered, and then nodded. It was only the

barest movement of her head, but it was enough. He dropped his mouth to hers and kissed her, letting her feel the full force of his desire. She groaned, the sound filling his mouth, resonating through him like the thrum of an engine reaching top speed. She belonged to him, and it was time to make his claim.

HANNA GAVE in to the need coursing through her, a flood of lust that washed away every rational thought in her head. The world started to whirl and spin as he kissed her, his hand stroking down her body until his fingers rested at the apex of her thighs. She bucked her hips in invitation, and after that, the world exploded into a maelstrom of sensations. His fingers found her clit, rubbing it with quick, circular motions that had her quivering in seconds, her breath coming in ragged gasps as he touched and teased her.

It didn't take him long to learn what she liked best, and soon she was riding the edge of a cresting wave that lifted her to the heights of bliss. When he slipped a finger into her slick channel, her body clamped around him eagerly, and when he added another finger and started fucking her with them, his thumb pressed to her clit, his mouth still mated to hers, she was lost.

She came as quietly as she could, her soft cries of pleasure muffled against his mouth as pleasure coursed through every cell in her body and she rode his fingers in mindless ecstasy.

"You are so beautiful," Jet's voice was thick with need as he withdrew his fingers from her body.

She blushed as she stared down at the hard body of her lover. He had the body of an athlete, all muscle and strength. He could have been sculpted from marble by a master artisan, and somehow, he was here, with her. "So are you."

He smiled as he guided her into position, one hand on her hip, the other on his cock. "I need you, *tani*."

"I'm yours." And in this one, perfect moment, she was.

"Here's where we find out if my research pays off," he joked as she settled over him, the impressively thick head of his cock pressing against her entrance.

"This is the easy part." She found herself smiling back at him as she took control, her eyes locked on his as she eased herself down onto his steel hard shaft.

He groaned her name as they came together, a long, drawn out sound of raw need that didn't stop until he was buried balls deep inside her. Her inner walls rippled around his length and she gasped as even the smallest movement made her body hum with pleasure.

Jet raised his legs, drawing his knees up to form a cradle for her body. He tangled one hand in her hair, pulling her in so close their breath mingled

"We are one," he said, his voice hushed but the words achingly clear. "I vow by the Flames of the First

One, to protect my mate, Hanna Dewan, from all who would do her harm. She will be my lover, my treasure, and my most cherished companion from now until we return to the Flame that birthed us."

She felt the weight of his words but stayed silent. She wasn't ready to commit to forever. After a handful of heartbeats, he closed the gap and kissed her, hard. She let herself be drawn into it, pushing aside thoughts of forever and embracing this moment. This, she could give him.

She set the pace, hands on his shoulders, holding tight as she rode him like one of the thoroughbred horses from the family stables. Every move he made, his muscles flexed and glided beneath her hands, and soon she was gripping him so tightly she knew she'd leave marks on his skin. She didn't care. In fact, she revelled in the idea of marking him, even if no one else would see it.

His kisses grew rougher, their pace more frantic as they chased each other towards release, every whisper of pleasure carefully muffled lest they be overheard. That fear added an extra edge to their lovemaking, and it wasn't long before she shuddered and came, burying her face in the crook of his neck to stifle her cry of pleasure.

He came a few seconds later, the heat of his orgasm filling her. Before he was done, she felt a change as his cock swelled, pressing against the most sensitive parts of her body and sending her tumbling into another orgasm.

When she had breath to speak again, she raised her head and rocked her hips against his still swollen cock. "Something you forgot to mention?"

Jet looked sheepish and smug at the same time. "During orgasm, I uh…swell. It locks us together for a little while."

"That's not all it does." She flexed her body around his cock, making him shudder and groan low in his throat. "This happens every time?"

"It does." He feathered several soft kisses against her mouth and cheeks. "That was incredible."

"It was." There wasn't any point in denying it. As she looked at him, she finally had enough of her wits about her to notice his eyes. Even in the dim light, she could see they were a brilliant shade of gold.

"Your eyes changed. I'll miss the blue, but I like gold, too. Does this mean you can conjure fire, now?"

He arched a dark brow at her. "Impatient, aren't you? I'm still waiting for my brain to start working again. Mostly all it's doing right now is saying 'mine, mine, mine' in an embarrassingly smug voice."

"The fire thing was the point of doing this, wasn't it?" She regretted the words the second they left her mouth. It wasn't the reason she'd said yes. It was the excuse she'd needed to give in to the Scorching.

His gold eyes narrowed. "Not for me, it wasn't. We're destined mates, Hanna. I know you did this because you feel you had to, and I'm sorry for that. But we're so much more than that. Why don't you believe it?"

"Because I don't believe in destiny. I can't. Too many people suffer too much for there to be some kind of cosmic plan to it all, at least on this planet." She shrugged. "I don't know, maybe if we had Gods like yours, it would be easier to believe, but ours don't speak to us. They don't grant us mates or magical powers."

Jet grinned. "No? I think you're wrong about that, *tani*." He reached up to tap two fingers on either side of her nose. "Your eyes changed colour, too. They are a stunning shade of gold."

"They are? What does that mean? How? I don't feel any different. Shouldn't I have felt that?"

"I didn't feel anything except the immense pleasure of being with you. It's possible we both missed something." His grin widened. "We were rather distracted."

"We were," She blushed as she agreed with him. "But what does it mean?"

Jet shrugged, the motion doing interesting things to his chest and shoulders. She had to force herself to stop staring and focus on what he was saying.

"Not many human females have manifested gold eyes. The few that have all developed the ability to conjure and control flame, just like a full-blooded Pyrosian."

"I can throw fireballs?" The idea both thrilled and terrified her.

"Maybe. We'll work on that soon, but before we do, we'll need to hang a blanket or something to block the light of the flames. Our guards might not be the brightest beings to walk this world, but they would certainly notice flames coming from inside our cells."

"They would." Her head was whirling as she tried to keep up with her thoughts and failed. There was too much to process, and all she really wanted to do was curl up in Jet's arms where she was warm and safe. Not that either of them were safe at the moment, and they wouldn't be until they got away from John and his fear-fueled army.

Jet folded her into his arms and held her tight. "You're thinking too much. Have faith that things will work out as they should, for all of us."

"I told you, I'm not much for faith, or Gods, or destiny."

He stroked her hair, kindling a fresh spark of desire in her breast. "I heard you, but that's not what I meant. You are the most intelligent, capable female I have met, on any planet. I meant that you should have some faith in yourself. We're going to get through this."

"How is it you always know the exact right thing to say?"

He chuckled and kissed the top of her head, a tender gesture that threatened to melt her heart completely.

"I'm a diplomat, *tani*. Knowing what to say and when to say it is pretty much my job description."

"And you're very good at it." She closed her eyes, determined to steal just a few more seconds of bliss. These moments might be all they had, and she wanted to make them last. Reality would return sooner than either of them would like. But when it did, they'd be ready.

CHAPTER SIX

IT HAD BEEN a long time since he'd spent an entire night cold and uncomfortable. It reminded Jet of his time in the military, though the company this time was a vast improvement over his former squad-mates.

They'd passed the time in a quiet cycle of lovemaking, talking, and then a bit of rest before the mating fever overcame them once again. Hanna would slip through the gap in the bars, naked and eager, only to retreat to her bunk once they could think clearly again. He knew it was necessary. They couldn't know when a guard might check on them, and the last thing they wanted was for their captors to realize that the thing they were most opposed to – a Pyrosian-human mating – had happened right under their noses. Valuable hostages or not, there was no way they'd escape unscathed if the truth came out.

The blankets worked to form a makeshift barrier so

he could practice summoning flame. It hadn't taken long for him to get the hang of it, though it would take more than a few hours to master his new talent.

Hanna hadn't managed more than a single spark, yet, despite hours of trying. The spark had flashed at the same time as her temper, but she'd been too tired to repeat the feat a second time. She would, though. It was inevitable. She was Pyrosian now.

She saw the changes in herself as another way to defend herself and her friend, Lily. He saw it as proof they were destined to be together despite her lingering doubts.

He rose from his bunk and stretched in a vain attempt to ease the stiffness in his limbs. Between rounds of mind-melting sex, the hard bunk, and the even harder floor, his body had grounds for complaint, but it was all worth it. Getting kidnapped was not a recommended way to meet your mate, but it had worked for him, and he'd never regret it. At least, not if everyone walked away when this ordeal ended.

Hanna sat up when he did, yawning as she ran her fingers through her sleep-tousled hair. Instantly his fingers itched to help, though he was certain that was part of how her hair had become tousled in the first place. He loved her hair, the warm weight of it in his hands, the subtle scent of her shampoo, the way he could wrap it around his fingers as he kissed her... He reined in his lust-muddled thoughts, but it was too late, his cock was hard as hull-plating again. It had only been an hour since they'd last made love. It was going to be a long, trying day.

"Did you sleep?" He asked softly.

"Not really. We should have just kept talking." She flashed him a tired smile. "I liked hearing about Pyros and what it was like to grow up there."

And he'd liked listening to her talk about her family, her work, and what had led her to create the Haven Network. Her file mentioned family members who had been killed, but now he knew the whole story. How her cousins and their mother had been caught in the middle of a war. Their home had been bombed, the city invaded, and they'd fled with nothing but the clothes they wore. They'd sent letters begging for help from her mother and promising to write once they reached safety. They'd never been heard from again.

"I liked talking to you, too. Hearing about your family, what happened to them. I've been thinking about ways to help as many females as we can get to Pyros so they can start over," he said.

"You want to start negotiating now? Here?" she raised her hands, her golden eyes gleaming with amusement. Her eyes were going to be a problem.

"No, *tani*. No negotiations. There's no need. We're a team now. We'll make this happen, together. And remember to keep your head down as much as you can. If anyone notices that your eyes have changed colours…"

She gestured to the gap they'd made in the bars. "Here's hoping they're not observant."

They had managed to prop the bar back into place, then covered it with the makeshift privacy curtain. It wasn't perfect, but it was all they could do.

They tidied themselves up as best they could, using hand wipes and a little of the water left from dinner. The level of activity was picking up in the warehouse, too. The lights came on, voices called to each other in greeting, and two unfamiliar males brought them breakfast in a pair of brown paper bags. The food was nondescript and greasy, but there was plenty of it, and this time, they'd brought him a meal, too.

"No coffee." Hanna lamented as she dug into her meal. "What do they think we're going to do, throw it at them?"

He grunted in commiseration. Unlike many of his brethren, he didn't like coffee, though he understood that it was a favourite among many humans, especially first thing in the morning. "If we were back at the embassy, I'd brew you a mug of *korta*. I think you'd like it."

"What's that?"

"A Romaki beverage with a nice, fruity flavour and a heart-slamming amount of caff— The rest of his words were drowned out by an earth-shattering roar that could only come from one source - a seriously pissed off dragon. Another roar sounded a few seconds later, sending the warehouse into total pandemonium.

He ran to his cell door to watch the chaos unfold while Hanna did the same on her side. "Is that what I think it is?" she asked.

"That is a Romaki dragon in a very bad mood. Our rescue is at hand."

They watched for a few more seconds, waiting for the area to clear out before they enacted their plan. Most of the Humanity First members ran in the same direction, but a small group were headed for the storage container where Lily and Vykor were imprisoned.

"Oh no." Hanna pointed to the group. "Is that John with them? What is he doing? Jet, quick. You have to get us out of here before he does something to Lily!"

A closer look at the group revealed why Hanna was worried. The men with John Ashton were heavily armed, wearing full tactical armour, and had almost identical expressions of grim determination on their faces. Whatever was about to happen, it wouldn't be good for Vykor or Lily.

Help might be coming, but it wasn't going to be here fast enough. He stepped back from the bars, raised his hands, and summoned his flames.

THIS SUCKS. She couldn't do a damned thing to help Lily. All she could do was watch in fear as the men approached Lily's prison. Chris and the other guard had disappeared, probably to defend their base. Voices were raised in panic, barking orders or screaming in fear. There was sporadic gunfire, muffled explosions, and occasionally, the bone-jarring roar of a dragon. She could almost swear there were two of them out there, but that didn't make sense. Jet had said Karos was the only other Romaki in the city.

She clung to the barred door, one eye on their captors, the other on her alien lover. Jet's outstretched hands were bathed in flames. They flew from his fingers to engulf the door to his cell. She could feel the heat radiating off of him, and she had to keep reminding herself that as his mate, the fire couldn't harm her.

The flames grew brighter, changing colour from red to orange to white. Near the end, the flames around his hands turned blue, but then the blaze grew so bright she had to shield her eyes.

Jet gave a cry of triumph a few seconds later, and the heat and light vanished. She lowered her hands to see the bars of his door glowing cherry red, the metal warped and bending in several places. He grabbed the loose bar from its spot near the wall and used it to push at the damaged door, ignoring the smoking ruins of his shirt sleeves. A few hard pushes and strikes with the bar destroyed what was left of the gate's integrity and the whole thing crashed to the ground.

She squeezed through the bars and raced to his side, leaving her shoes behind. They'd only slow her down. Jet tossed away the metal bar, scooped her into his arms, and charged through the still glowing doorway.

She pulled her arms and legs in tight, but she still got burns on her legs and feet as he carried her out of their prison. It was a small price to pay to be free.

The second he was past the destroyed gate, he set her down, and they took off running for the far side of the warehouse. The group was inside the other shipping container now, and over the chaos and noise of the fight outside she heard Lily screaming in fury.

"Stay behind me!" Jet reminded her as they closed the distance. They'd talked about this, too. His flames wouldn't hurt her, but they would hurt anyone else, including their friends. He needed a clear line of sight to avoid harming them by accident.

"No!" They were close enough now she could hear what Lily was screaming. "This is insane. You're insane! I'm not going anywhere with you."

"Leave her. I'll go, but only if you leave her here where it's safe. You only need one hostage. Take me." That had to be Vykor.

They were only a few strides from the door when Lily cried out. Then there was a gunshot that tore Hanna's hopes to shreds. *No!*

That was when it all went to hell. Someone bellowed in rage and grief, the sound starting out human but morphing into something far larger and fiercer. It battered at her senses and made the floor beneath them shudder.

Jet stopped dead, throwing out his arms to catch her as she raced by him. "Get back. Now!"

He turned and ran back the way they'd come, dragging her with him.

"But Lily!"

The container started to buckle. Something huge tore it apart from the inside.

"Move!"

The steel walls of the shipping container shredded like tissue paper, and a creature from out of legend rose from the wreckage. She was looking at a dragon.

"He's purple?" Hanna barely recognized her own voice.

"Apparently." Jet wrapped an arm around her waist and tucked her in close to his side.

"That's not one of the usual colours." She was babbling and she knew it, but she couldn't seem to stop talking.

"No. He's something new." They watched in fascination as Vykor stepped out of the wreckage, then turned and blasted his former prison with a blast of fire that turned the entire container to molten slag, along with everyone still inside.

"Where's Lily! Oh god, did he kill her?" She raised her voice. "Hey, dragon! What the hell did you do with my friend?"

Vykor's head snapped up and he stared at her for a long, terrifying second. Then he raised his head, snorted in irritation, and unfurled his wings to reveal Lily lying face down across his back.

She didn't move, and Hanna's fear returned tenfold. "Lily!"

She tried to run toward Vykor and his precious burden, but Jet wouldn't let her go. "Stop, Hanna. We need to stay clear."

"Clear of what?"

Vykor swung his massive head around so he was facing the wall, then exhaled a cloud of crystalline vapour that enveloped the entire area, covering everything it touched in a layer of shimmering frost. Then he spun and slammed his tail into the wall. There was a cacophony of screeching metal and tumbling masonry, and most of the wall gave way, creating an escape route.

"Clear of *that*." Jet sounded slightly awed.

Vykor ambled through the gap he'd made, shielding Lily with his wings as he walked past the still crumbling edges of the hole. She and Jet followed, picking their way carefully through the debris. The cold bit at her feet but she didn't say anything. All she wanted was to get to Lily and find out if she was alright.

Outside, the overcast sky was a damp and ruffled grey and the wind carried the scent of the sea, along with the promise of rain. A dragon roared above them and she looked up in time to see a crimson beast the size of a tour bus hurtling toward the ground. She expected it to land gracefully, but instead it hit hard, skidding across the concrete and taking out a wall of a neighbouring warehouse.

"*That's* Karos?" She asked.

"No. I have no idea who that lunatic is." Jet pointed to where a second red dragon, even larger than the first, set down. "That's Karos."

The larger dragon draped a wing over the smaller one in a protective gesture. "Oi, Romaki dragonmen, Lily needs help over here!"

As strange as the last twenty-four hours had been, seeing two mythological creatures shimmer and transform into ordinary people ranked pretty high on her list. Especially when one of the dragons turned into her friend, Megan.

She stared while Jet laughed.

As Megan and the huge Romaki male sprinted towards them, Hanna finally found her voice. "Megan. What the hell is going on, and why can you turn into a dragon?"

CHAPTER SEVEN

"I'm so sorry, *tani*. I forgot you weren't wearing shoes." Jet stood beside Hanna and held her hand as a Pyrosian medical officer tended to her injured feet. She'd been badly cut exiting the building, and he hadn't noticed. She'd been burned, too, and hadn't said anything. He'd promised to protect her, and failed to live up to his word. He needed her trust, and so far, he'd done a lousy job of proving himself worthy of it. Now they were free, he'd have to do better.

"We got out. That's all that matters." She glanced over to the vehicle where more medical officers were working on Lily. Vykor had refused to step away, and after his dragon growled at the staff, they stopped trying to move him.

Jet understood how Vykor must be feeling. There wasn't a force in the galaxy that could make him leave Hanna's side.

Vykor wasn't the only one sticking close to Lily. A massive canine lay nearby, watching whatever was going on inside the vehicle with solemn eyes, its wide head resting on its paws.

Hanna had recognized the beast, which had appeared as Vykor handed Lily's unconscious body over to the medics. Vykor had called the beast Cupcake and said it was Lily's, and no one seemed inclined to interfere with either the dog or the dragon as they stood watch over their female.

Only after Hanna had been treated and provided with borrowed footwear did he allow himself to be checked over. They treated his bruises, handed them each a bottle of water, a blanket, and sent them on their way with a reminder to stay hydrated and eat something soon. The only thing he was hungry for was Hanna, but he couldn't start that feast until they were back at the embassy. He couldn't wait to get home to a soft bed, a hot shower, room service, and a door that only locked from the inside.

They drank their water and tried to get close enough to the vehicle where Lily was being treated to glean something about her condition, but they were shooed away.

"Can't you tell me how she's doing? Please, she's my friend."

The medic started to shake her head, then sighed. "I can't tell you much, but she's holding on. We should know more soon."

"She has to be alright." Hanna's voice quavered as she looked up at him, and he felt her worry like a physical blow. It was the first time he'd sensed her emotions, and it faded a second later, but he knew what he'd felt. Their bond was strong and getting stronger.

"She will be. Pyrosian medicine is far more advanced than human. She'll be fine," he said, hoping like hell the Gods weren't going to make him a liar. If her friend didn't make it, Hanna would carry the grief and guilt for the rest of her life.

There was still plenty to concern them all, but the Humanity First movement wasn't one on the list. Not anymore.

Most of the true believers had died defending their base, leaving just the petty thugs and guns for hire alive. The mercenary types had given up the first chance they could and were on their way to police headquarters to be charged and processed. Chris, the chocolate smuggling cell guard, had survived. Jet had seen him being placed into a vehicle, hands cuffed, shoulders slumped in defeat. Kyle had survived, too. He'd been caught trying to sneak away after the fighting ended.

Keth and Eva, the mated pair who ran the embassy, were busy speaking with reporters, telling them a well-crafted version of events that would ensure that public opinion turned against the Humanity First group. Keth had stopped by for a few minutes to make sure both he and Hanna were alright, and Jet had taken the opportunity to convey a few key pieces of information, including the way John and the others had treated their human captives. The fact that Vykor confirmed that John had been the one to shoot Lily only added more weight to the argument that the Firsters were less concerned about human rights and more about fomenting fear through whatever means necessary, including murder.

"If we can't get more information, then we should go see Megan." Hanna brightened at the mention of her friend's name. "I still haven't heard how she wound up a dragon, or how they found us, and I'm certain she thinks this is all her fault and needs to apologize."

"Her and Karos, both." There'd been no time to speak during the frantic rush to get Lily seen to, but he'd seen the look in his friend's eyes. Karos was convinced he was to blame for everything.

They held hands for the short walk to the others, but the moment Hanna saw Megan she let go of him to hug her friend. He let her go, but he didn't like watching her walk away. They belonged together, and once he got her back to the embassy, he was going to prove it to her.

SHE HUGGED Megan hard and hung onto her as they both babbled happily. Megan kept trying to apologize, and it was hard not to laugh as she struggled to speak past her newly developed fangs. *Fangs.* Megan had fangs because she was a dragon. It was going to take some time to wrap her head around that.

Hanna put a stop to Megan's apologies with another hug. "You didn't fail me. You came back for us. As a dragon! How did that happen?" Hanna glanced over at the large, red-haired male standing with Jet. "Or can I guess?"

"You're one to talk." Megan grinned and pointed to Hanna's eyes. "You and the diplomat, huh?"

Hanna nodded, slightly embarrassed to admit it. "I know he's too young for me, but when we touched there was a spark. *The* spark. It made it impossible to think clearly, and I thought if we gave in, he'd have his fire powers and we could use that to escape." She sighed. "Not that it worked out that way."

Megan gave her a knowing look. "You're making excuses. Stop it. Believe me, I did it too, but if the Scorching is anything like the fucking *rux*, you didn't have a choice." She lowered her voice. "It's like some kind of sexual insanity."

"You, too?"

Megan grinned. "Uh huh. Karos says it's going to go on for another day or so, too. I get moments of clarity, but then my brain turns to mush again."

"Same. But are you happy? Will you stay with him?"

She knew the answer the moment her friend looked at the Romaki male. There was more than lust in Megan's expression, there was happiness, and a deep satisfaction that suited the other woman.

"He's my mate. Destiny, divine meddling, fate, however you want to put it, he's the one for me." Megan tapped her temple. "And my dragon thinks so, too."

"It's really like that? You have another voice in your head?"

"Yep, and she's loud. Bossy, too. Can't imagine where she gets that from."

Hanna couldn't help it, she laughed and hugged Megan again. "I'm sure I don't know."

She had so many questions, but before she could ask any of them Megan asked one of her own. "What happened to Lily?"

"John shot her." Vykor had told them that much.

Megan growled, and there was more than a little of her dragon present in the sound. "I still can't believe her asshole half-brother was behind all this. I thought he was back in prison."

"We all did. He tried to make us think Lily was working with him, too. I don't know what he thought that would accomplish. The only one who might know is Lily, and she's in no condition to talk right now."

"She's going to be alright though, isn't she? I mean, the Pyrosians can fix her up?"

"They're doing their best."

"If Vykor hadn't already killed her bastard of a brother, I'd happily tear his head off right now. How did he die, anyway? No one's said anything."

"Incinerated him, I think, but I'm not sure. We were

too slow getting out of our cells to help. By the time we got to them, Lily had been shot and Vykor had gone full Smaug."

Megan's brows rose to her dark hairline. "Did you just make a Hobbit reference? When did you start watching fantasy movies?"

"Have you seen the guys they cast to play the dwarves in those films? They gave me an appreciation for men with beards." She glanced at Jet and blushed as a fresh surge of lust rolled through her. As far as she was concerned, Jet put every actor and model she'd ever seen to shame. Suddenly the distance between them felt enormous, and she took a half-step toward him. She needed to be closer, to touch him, feel his arms wrapped around...

Megan snickered. "Yeah, I can see that."

Before she could say anything else, there was a happy shout from the ambulance area, and Cupcake the hellhound started barking madly.

"Who brought a dog?" Megan asked.

"She's with Lily. It's a long story." Yet another tale she didn't know the details of, because she'd been distracted by Jet instead of trying to communicate with Lily somehow. She should have done more. Tried harder to escape. If she had, then maybe Lily wouldn't have gotten hurt.

"Well, sounds like she's going to be okay. Do you think we should check on her?"

Hanna shook her head. "They sent us packing the

last time we tried, but they did say they'd give us news when they had it. Hopefully someone comes by soon to let us know how she's doing."

They didn't have to wait long. Vykor joined them within a few minutes, and he carried Lily in his arms.

Hanna hadn't spent much time with the young Romaki male, but it was evident that he'd changed more than his clothes since they'd parted company. He carried himself more confidently and smiled at everyone. He was dressed in a dark blue outfit that looked nothing like the suit he'd worn yesterday. It was loose and made from a fabric she didn't recognize. It took her several seconds for it to dawn on her that Vykor must have used magic to create new clothes. *Handy trick.*

Lily was dressed in something similar, though the colour was a vibrant violet that matched her eyes, which were shining with unabashed delight as she spotted everyone and started waving. "I'm okay."

Relief filled her as she and Megan ran to see Lily, the three of them hugging and catching each other up on what they'd experienced. It amused her that Vykor held Lily the entire time, refusing her occasional requests to put her down.

Megan kept apologizing and Lily repeatedly assured them that she had no part in her brother's schemes. There was laughter, reassurances, and explanations, though not nearly enough to answer all her questions.

So much had happened, and now, everything had changed.

Jet and Karos rejoined them, and when Jet draped an arm across her shoulders, she leaned into his embrace, craving the comfort of his touch. His fingers moved over her in slow, seductive circles, and she knew he was as affected by the Scorching as she was. Karos had his arms around Megan, and it was soon apparent that a longer reunion would have to wait until they were clear of the lust-inducing madness they'd all been infected with.

She wanted more time with her friends, but she couldn't hold onto her relief that they were alright, nor her frustration at how brief their time together was. Her thoughts were like soap bubbles drifting past. If she tried to focus on one for too long, it burst and was gone. Megan said it was the same for her, but she didn't seem to mind. In fact, Megan was almost glowing with contentment, and Lily was radiantly happy. Whatever they were going through, neither of them had a moment's doubt about their destined mates. *So, why am I still not sure?* Jet was amazing. Smart. Warm-hearted. Handsome as hell, and on top of all that, he'd turned out to be a generous and talented lover.

You know what the problem is. A cruel voice whispered from the back of her mind. Jet was still young enough he should want children, a family of his own. That was the whole purpose for which the Star-Crossed Dating

Agency had been created - to pair young Pyrosian males with human women so they rebuilt their population. He couldn't have that with her. After suffering the agonizing pain of endometriosis for more than a decade she'd opted for a hysterectomy. She'd been over forty and had known for years she didn't want children. She didn't regret her choice, but Jet might. Destined mates or not, he needed to know. Once he did, he'd likely change his mind about wanting forever with her.

Jet's lips brushed her ear and she lost her train of thought.

"I need you, *tani*. Soon."

His words made her shiver while her pussy clenched and flooded with arousal. She gave him a tiny nod, then raised her voice so the others could hear her. "We should—" Jet's hand cupped her ass and she broke off with a blush.

"I need to go with Vykor," Lily agreed, almost whispering the words.

"Karos and I should go, too," Megan said.

"But we're coming back. Right?" Lily asked worriedly.

"Of course." The words came automatically, but Hanna wasn't sure it was entirely true. They'd all be back together again, but things had changed so much she wasn't sure the three of them would ever be the same.

They said their goodbyes, and Hanna watched in amazement as Vykor, Karos, and Megan shifted to their dragon forms. Lily rode on Vykor's back, swaddled in so many warm clothes and blankets she was barely visible.

She watched the sky until they vanished from sight, then turned in Jet's arms so she could see his face. "Let's go."

He kissed her gently, reining in the desire she could see blazing in his eyes. "Finally. I get to take you home."

IT WAS ALL he could do not to take her in the back of the town car on the way back to the embassy. When she went to buckle in, he'd pulled her into his lap instead, unwilling to let her sit so far away. His need for her was making him crazy, and once he got her behind locked doors, he wasn't going to let her out of his sight for days.

Maybe by then his mind would clear enough he could think about other things, like the fact his friends had found their mates and the Humanity First movement had been crushed. He wanted to rejoice in those facts, but he couldn't focus on anything except Hanna.

Since the moment of the Spark, she'd become the center of his orbit. He loved the way she tasted, the soft warmth of her touch, the sound of her laughter, the soft moan she made just before she came. Flames, he loved everything about her. She was everything he didn't know was missing from his life.

He ran his hands through her hair, using it to hold her close as he kissed her again and again.

There was a throng of news vans, cameramen, and reporters surrounding the embassy. Protected by the tinted windows that kept them hidden from view, neither of them said anything as their driver eased them through the crowd and past the gate. He was grateful to Keth, who would be handling the media for the next few days. The embassy had adopted the Pyrosian military's stance that no staff member was to report to work while under the influence of the Scorching. He only had one focus for the next few days, and she was nestled in his lap, staring out the window in bemused silence. Her emotions were strong enough for him to feel but too tangled for him to make sense of.

"What is it, _tani_?"

"I was thinking I should get a statement out to the press, but all my staff have flown away. I knew things would change, but it hadn't occurred to me that they already have."

"Our staff will help with everything. They've already reached out to your office in Toronto to update them on your status. They can let your family know you're alright, too. Later, we'll worry about statements and the media. We escaped. Everyone's alive and well. It's time to celebrate."

Hanna gave him a knowing look, her lush lips

turned up into a smile. "You just want to get me naked again."

"That's where you're wrong, my beautiful mate. Until now, circumstances haven't allowed us the luxury of getting properly naked. I intend to correct this tragic state of affairs as soon as possible."

"First naked. Then into a hot shower."

The thought of sharing a shower with her had him hard in seconds and he had to fight the urge to groan aloud. "Whatever my mate wishes."

She shivered and kissed him, her hands fisted in his shirt as she pulled him close. "Until this Scorching passes, all I wish for is time alone with you."

That was a wish he would happily fulfill.

CHAPTER EIGHT

HANNA COULDN'T REMEMBER a time she'd indulged in so much decadence. Over the last few days she'd surrendered completely to the Scorching. She'd given in to desires so primal she blushed every time she thought about what they'd done to and with each other. She was still concerned about their age difference, but she couldn't deny that having a younger lover certainly had some advantages. In fact, the last few days had been so good, she was starting to think things might actually work out between them.

This morning they'd both woken to find their minds were finally clearing, and their desire for each other, while still strong, wasn't overpowering. The mating fever was fading, which meant it was time to face reality.

They hadn't talked about the future much since being freed. Instead, they'd talked about other things, their childhoods, family, their homes. She told him about the countries she'd visited and the people she'd met, first with her parents, and later on her own as she started the Haven Network. He was fascinated by her stories of the mining operations her father had taken her to see, and she was just as interested in his tales of distant planets, alien species, and life in the Pyrosian court.

Whatever her future with Jet might be, she was more determined than ever to visit Pyros. Once she'd seen it for herself, she believed it could be a safe haven for so many refugees. Jet believed it, too. She'd sensed it when they'd talked. Their bond was stronger now. She could feel his presence even when he wasn't in the room, and if she focused, she could catch glimmers of his emotions, and he could sense hers, as well. If they weren't meant to be together, surely their bond wouldn't be so strong?

She held out a hand and snapped her fingers, summoning a flame that engulfed her hand. She watched it burn for a moment, then willed it away again. The flame. Her eyes. The link between them. It all led her to the same conclusion.

The two of them could have a life together.

She finished dressing, thankful someone had the foresight to retrieve her luggage from the wrecked limousine and bring it to the embassy. Not that she'd needed much in the way of clothing the last few days. They hadn't left Jet's quarters once, and limited their communications to voice only when they spoke to the other couples. She had talked often to Megan and Lily, though never for long.

The only time she'd worn clothes was while a couple of Pyrosian techs had visited to set her up with a cognitive augmentation package. She'd dozed for a few hours, and when she woke, her head was full of new facts and languages. It was amazing, just like everything else in Jet's world.

She looked around Jet's bedroom one last time. It was comfortable but not opulent, with an understated elegance that matched the man who lived here. Cream-coloured walls, thick rugs over polished wood floors, and furnishings that could have come from any high-end store. The familiar comforts were combined with advanced technologies. View screens that mimicked windows with ever-changing views, a fleet of service droids and robots that did everything from sweep the floor to deliver their meals. They were belowground, but the air was fresh, the lighting so natural it was hard to remember the fact.

"You're stalling," she scolded herself. She hadn't told him the details of her infertility, yet, and the more she started to believe they had a chance of being happy, the more she dreaded telling him. Every scenario that played through her mind ended with anger, disappointment, and heartache.

Still, she couldn't put it off any longer. She'd just have to do something she never imagined doing: have faith in a higher power. She closed her eyes, ignored how foolish she felt, and whispered, "Jet believes this is all part of your plan. I'm not sure I believe in you…but I do trust him. So, if you're out there, I could use a hand with this next part. And uh, if this mating was your doing? Thank you."

She opened her eyes and went looking for her mate. Jet had gone to his private office to catch up on work while she showered and got herself together. His office was off the main living area, and the moment she opened the bedroom door she heard his voice. He was speaking in Pyrosian, and he sounded pissed.

"I know your feelings on this, Father. You've made them very clear."

Another voice, louder and as hard as granite, answered. "Excellent. Then your mother and I will expect you and your new mate to return to Pyros shortly. Our grandchildren will be raised here, of course. They'll need to make the right friends, receive all the best training. We'll start making arrangements."

"You need to listen to me. Your grandchildren—"

"You'll have to let your mother know when you're arriving. She'll arrange a proper reception, and she'll want to introduce your…what did you say the human's name was?"

"Her name is Hanna." Jet was almost snarling in frustration, now, and his anger battered her through their bond.

Damn it. They were talking about *grandchildren.* She

shouldn't have waited to tell Jet the truth. Now his parents were expecting him to come home and start a family. A family she couldn't give him. He was arguing with them over a future they'd never have.

She froze in place, torn between guilt, shame, and a desire to stand with him as he fought to make his father understand things had changed. Jet had told her about his plans to live by his own rules, free of his family's obligations and expectations. She'd encouraged him. But now, she had to let him fight this battle alone because anything she could say would only make things worse.

Jet's father kept talking, but she didn't want to hear anymore. Later, she'd come back and tell Jet the truth. She'd wasted her breath asking for divine aid. If they existed at all, they weren't going to help her. With her friends gone, there was no one in her corner. She was on her own, and if that was the case, then she needed some time alone so she could think.

Slipping past the office door unseen, she let herself out of Jet's quarters and into the corridor. She was so focused on getting out quietly, she almost tripped over the package outside the door.

"And wouldn't that have been an end to my stealthy escape." She picked up the brown paper package. It was solid and had some weight to it, and her name was written on it in purple marker, along with a single line of instructions. "Open me."

She walked down the hall until she found an empty

alcove before unwrapping the gift. Inside was a book and a note. The book was one she recognized. Hell, just about every woman on the planet knew this book. "What to expect when your mate is an alien," was an international bestseller, co-written by two human women, Aria Frasier and Haley Anderson.

The note was written in the same purple marker. "Come find me when you get this. Eva." There was a room number and directions scrawled beneath the name.

She didn't feel like going on a scavenger hunt, but she didn't have anywhere else to go, so she tucked the book under her arm and followed the directions to an office on the main floor of the embassy. She knocked on the metal door and it slid open, revealing a cozy office done in soft pastel shades.

Eva looked up from her desk with a smile. "Hi. I was wondering when you'd appear. Come in. Can I get you anything? Tea? Coffee? Have you tried *korta* yet? It's delicious."

"Uh, hi. Coffee would be great." Eva's natural effervescence set her at ease, and she came into the room and took a seat, placing the book on the cluttered desk. "Thanks for the gift, by the way."

Eva was already on her feet and pouring coffee into a bright pink mug. "You're welcome. We keep a bunch of them on hand to give out to newly mated females. Things were so crazy before, no one thought to give you one."

"I'm not sure I was in any condition to read it, anyway. By the time I got here, things were sort of past that point."

Eva laughed and set down the mug, along with cream and sugar. "Oh believe me, I remember. Keth and I had a rough start, too. I was so badly injured in the stadium bombing it took me forever to wake up. By that time, they'd had to put Keth under to protect him from the effects of the Scorching. He almost lost me, then I almost lost him, and then *hoo* boy, the Scorching took us both."

"But it all worked out for the two of you." She was too tense to relax, but she sipped the coffee to give herself something to do.

"Of course it did. We're true mates. That doesn't mean it was easy." She shook her blonde head and laughed. "The males all seem to think it's going to be simple. No matter how many training sessions we give them, they're always surprised when it doesn't all fall into place." Eva reached over to tap the book. "Which is why my friends wrote that."

It was all a little surreal. Here she was, drinking coffee and chatting with a near stranger about being mated to an alien. Still, Eva was the only woman she knew in this entire place, and she was mated to a Pyrosian, too. "So, I'm not the only one to have doubts?"

Eva got up and walked over to her. "May I hug you? I think you need it."

Hanna nodded and Eva gave a small coo of delight and hugged her. "It's going to be okay. This is what we call stage two. Also known as the 'what the hell am I doing?' stage. Almost everyone goes through it, especially those of us who found their mates accidentally."

Eva returned to her side of the desk and plopped herself down in her chair. "So, what's worrying you?"

"Everything. I mean, I like Jet. A lot. He's sweet and smart and always knows exactly what to say to make me laugh, and he did his best to protect me when we were taken, but I don't really know him at all." Once the words started coming, they poured out of her in a flood she couldn't stop. "And then there's the age difference. I mean, he's a decade younger than me. He should be with someone his own age. Someone who could give him a…" She finally stopped herself from talking.

Eva was silent for a long moment, then folded her hands on the desk and leaned forward. "No one is saying you have to be in love with him already. The Scorching is intense, but it's not love. Oh, they think it is, but they've had their whole lives to come to terms with the Spark thing. Touch a girl, get the spark, poof! You're mated." She threw up her hands. "It takes us humans a little longer, but so far, every woman who's met her mate has fallen in love with him eventually."

"All of them?"

"All of them. No matter what their differences."

"And how many of them couldn't have children? I mean, that's the whole point of the Pyrosians coming here, right?" She hadn't meant to toss the words out like a challenge, but that's how it sounded, even to her.

Eva sat back in her chair, her hands pulled in close to her stomach. "That's not a common issue. In fact, I only know of one pairing like that."

"One?" Hanna had expected her to say there hadn't been any. "And they're still together?"

"Oh yes." Eva's smile returned. "They're together, and very much in love. We're hoping to adopt a baby eventually, but it's a bit complicated what with Keth being from another planet and all."

Her train of thought jumped the track and landed in a tangled, smoking heap. "Wait. What? You?"

"Can't have children," Eva confirmed. "Cancer."

"I'm so sorry. I didn't know."

"There's nothing to be sorry for. Not every woman is destined for motherhood. I'm alive, I have a life and a male I love. It's more than enough."

"And Keth doesn't care? Isn't he supposed to?"

"You've been reading too much of our propaganda. It's true, to a point, but it's not the whole truth." Eva grinned. "I mean, when have you ever met a group of people who are all in agreement about everything, never mind an entire planet?"

Eva had a point, but there was a bigger problem. "When I left, Jet was speaking to his father. It uh, wasn't going well, so I didn't stay to listen long, but I heard enough. His family are expecting him to bring his mate home so our children can be raised on Pyros."

Eva's eyes widened. "Ah. And what did Jet say to that?"

"I don't know. I left." She winced at her own words. Why had she left instead of waiting for Jet's response? She was a grown woman, and she'd run away like a child who didn't want to hear the word no.

"Does he know where you are right now?" Eva asked, trying not to smirk.

"No. I uh…"

Eva giggled. "You snuck out? Oh, man. You are *so* in stage two right now. It happens a lot. Which is why I left the book. Do you think he's going to come looking for you any time soon? Should we tell him where you are?"

Hanna shifted her focus to the bond she shared with Jet. He was still radiating anger and frustration, and she got the sense that he was still in his office, dealing with his father. "He's still busy dealing with his father. We should have some time."

Eva nodded and picked up a communicator, tapping a few keys. "I'm letting Keth know you're with me. He'll let Jet know. And now, since we have a little time, I think you and I should make some calls. It's time you talked to the others."

The others? She didn't want to talk to anyone right now. Her friends were all away, and her family loved her, but they hadn't understood her life or her choices in years.

"Maggie, Gwen, Aria. Maybe Hayley and Lisa, if they're not busy with their babies."

"You mean Maggie Pyr, the princess?"

"I do. You wanted to talk to them about life on Pyros, right? As part of your plans for the Haven Network. And I think talking to them will help you feel better about what's happened to you. So, we're just going to take out two ships with one comet." Eva beamed. "Easy peasy."

"Easy?" she laughed. "I've forgotten what that is. Nothing's been easy since I got kidnapped and discovered my mate was also my cellmate."

"It gets better. I promise."

Hanna relaxed into her chair, cradling her mug in her hands. She wasn't sure talking to the other women would help her, but it couldn't hurt.

JET REACHED the end of his patience. He'd listened to his father lecture and pontificate on all the reasons he needed to come back to Pyros. He'd heard it all before, but his father recited every item as if it was the first time they'd ever discussed it. He might have been able to ignore it, but then his sire had started in on Hanna. Calling her the human female, questioning her suitability, and making it clear he expected grandchildren as soon as possible, another generation he could indoctrinate and control the same way they controlled him. He wouldn't let that happen.

"Enough!" He shouted at the screen.

"What did you say to me?"

"I said enough. As in shut the hell up and listen to me. For once in your life, listen!"

"You will not speak to me in that tone of voice."

"Why not? It's the same tone you're using on me." Jet squared his shoulders and faced his father. "I'm not a child, anymore. I'm a grown male with a mate and a life of my own."

"You're a Tindor, and my heir. Your life isn't your own. Never has been."

"That was true before, but it's not true anymore. I'm done, father. I'm staying on Earth with Hanna. We'll visit Pyros, but that's all it will be - a visit." Spending time with Hanna, talking about their childhoods and families, it had brought a new perspective to things. He'd run away, but it wasn't enough. He needed to make a clean break.

"But your children! You can't possibly think to raise them on that primitive planet?"

"Who said anything about having children?"

"But…you're mated!" the old man sputtered.

"Yes, I am. That doesn't mean I want to be a father. You assumed it, just like you assumed everything else about me." He slammed his hand against his thigh.

"You don't know me at all." Gods, it felt good to finally admit it.

"I know that if you don't stop this insanity, I'll have no choice but to disown you. You'll be on your own. No money. No family influence. No political capital."

He lifted his chin and met his father's gaze. "If that's what you need to do."

For several long seconds they stared at each other. Then his father's eyes widened and he looked away. "We'll discuss this later. Clearly the Scorching is still addling your brain." His father cut off the transmission with an angry wave of his hand and the screen went black.

Jet spun on his heel and left his office, still seething. He went straight to their bedroom, looking for Hanna. She had to have heard the argument, or at least felt his anger through their bond, and he wanted to explain what had happened. Only she wasn't there.

"Hanna?" Her suitcase still sat in the corner, her brush was on the bedside table, but she was nowhere to be seen. "Hanna, where are you?"

Where the flames had she gone? He hadn't even heard her leave. He focused on the link between them and exhaled in relief when he sensed her nearby and happy.

Laughing? Who was she laughing with? A surge of jealousy hit him, proving that his father was right about one thing, the Scorching hadn't faded completely, yet. Probably why he'd had the courage to stand up for himself...or maybe it was because of Hanna. Meeting her had shown him what it truly meant to have a mission, a purpose. She'd dedicated her life to helping others. Now, he intended to spend his life helping her achieve her dreams.

He chuckled in a moment of wry self-awareness. He should probably tell her about that at some point. He'd spent so much time trying to show her that they belonged together, he'd failed to mention what he wanted out of their life. Maybe because until he met her, he hadn't really known what it was.

He picked up a communicator, then belatedly realized it wouldn't be helpful. He hadn't gotten one for Hanna, yet. Instead, he contacted Keth. The male oversaw the embassy. If anyone could help him find his mate, it would be him.

"Finally figured out she wasn't in your rooms?" Keth said by way of greeting.

"In my defence, I was rather busy picking a fight with my father. In other news, I think I might be about to get disowned."

Keth chuckled. "Should I be offering you condolences or congratulations?"

"Just tell me I still have a job, and then tell me where my mate is. I take it you know her location."

"Of course you still have a job. I've had to do it the last few days, and honestly, you can come back to work any time now. Talking to the media is exhausting. Oh, and Hanna is in Eva's office. She's been talking to some of the human females on Pyros. Something about stage two?"

Unlike most males, Jet had read the book. He was asked about it during so many interviews he'd had to. "Stage two? That's…not good."

He checked the link between them again. She was still happy and not at all distressed. So what was Keth talking about?

"A word of advice from a mated male. If things aren't good, that's no time to be leaving your female alone."

"Very helpful," he replied dryly.

"Consider it payback for making me do your job for the last three days. Now go find your mate so you can learn one of the truly great benefits to being mated."

"What's that?"

"The humans call it make-up sex."

"Got it. I'm going to find Hanna now." He ended the call and made for the door. He needed to find her, fix whatever had upset her enough to make her leave their room, get her naked, and learn what make-up sex was all about.

CHAPTER NINE

HANNA'S TIME with Eva and the others had been both enlightening and uplifting. Megan and Lily had joined in for part of the conversation, too. They'd reaffirmed the plans they'd made, reassuring her that despite the changes in all their lives, some things were still the same. They were still a team.

She hadn't wanted to end it so soon, but she'd sensed Jet's mood had changed. She couldn't explain how, but she knew he was looking for her.

The others had nodded and laughed in understanding. Eva had programmed a communicator for her, one that had all their contact information so she could reach out any time she needed to.

"And believe me, you'll need to," Gwen had said with a mischievous smile. "I love Kash more than anything, but in the beginning…"

Maggie laughed. "In the beginning, Gwen set Kash's room on fire."

"And I crashed Vadir's ship!" Lisa added proudly.

"And I walked out on Tarjen, which wasn't terribly practical, considering we were in orbit at the time," Aria confessed.

"And I might have accused Torel of human experimentation and set myself on fire," Haley said.

Their laughter followed her into the corridor, and she smiled as she retraced her steps. The other women's support and advice had helped her find her center again and renewed her feelings of hope. Jet's Gods had come through for her after all.

She was only a few steps away from his door when Jet strode out into the hall. "Hanna!"

"Hi. Sorry I left. I heard you arguing with your father, and I –"

He cut her off by hauling her into his arms and kissing her until she forgot what she'd been saying.

"So, you missed me then?" She asked when he finally let her up for air.

"Always." He touched his chest. "If I hadn't been able to sense that you were alright, I might have torn this place apart looking for you."

She placed her hand over his. "I could feel you, too. I wanted to be there for you, but..."

He bowed his head and kissed her again, a slow, tender kiss that made her want to lean into his strength and stop talking altogether. "Why did you leave?"

"Inside." She said, pushing lightly at his chest. This wasn't a conversation she wanted to have in public.

He lifted her into his arms and carried her.

"I can walk!"

"I know. But this is more fun." He carried her over to the small sitting area inside, then sat with her on his lap.

"So?" He prompted her.

"How did things end with your family?" *Way to duck the question.*

"Messy. There's a good chance I'm about to be disowned." He made the announcement with a grin.

"You don't seem overly concerned about that."

"I'm not. I thought coming to Earth would be enough to make them understand I'm done living my life by their rules. I should have stated that clearly instead of running away. Now, they know. They're not happy about it, but that's their problem, not mine. I have my own money, a job I enjoy, friends I cherish, and you. What else do I need?"

She wouldn't get a better opening than this. "What about children?"

His golden eyes widened. "What about them? Is that why you left? You heard my father going on about raising our younglings on Pyros?"

"He seemed pretty adamant."

"He always does." Jet stroked her cheek gently. "I can feel how upset you are right now. What is it, my *tani*?"

"I can't have children."

She waited, watching his reaction. Instead of retreating, or even frowning, he offered her a smile that melted her heart.

"Okay."

"That's it? I tell you I'm infertile and you say okay? Like it's no big deal."

"I told you I was probably going to be disowned, and you barely blinked. No Pyrosian female would have taken the news so well."

"But I have money. Why would I want yours?"

He chuckled and snuggled her in tight to his chest, tucking her head beneath his chin as he held her. "Flames, you are so perfect for me."

"Except for the no kids thing."

"No. You're perfect. Period. I decided a long time ago that I didn't want a mate or children. I couldn't imagine watching my father do to them what he did to my brother and me." He hugged her again. "I thought that being mated to you meant I might need to reconsider. After all, it's my job to promote the idea of every male needing a mate and a family of my own."

"You didn't want to be mated?" His words should have worried her, but they didn't. Now when he was holding her in his arms and she could feel how much he cared for her. He'd been right about that. Pyrosian matings weren't anything like human relationships. They were so much more.

"Not until I found you. That's when I realized that I

could have a mate who wanted the same things I did. We were made to complement each other, *tani*. In every way. I don't need more than that."

She exhaled as something deep inside her finally released. "I should have said something earlier. It would have saved me so much worry."

He nuzzled her hair. "You did, though. You told me that your marriage ended because he expected you to stay home and be a wife and mother. That was never what you wanted. It isn't who you are. I'm the one who should have said something."

"I can't believe you remember that. Do all Pyrosian men listen as well as you do?"

"I'm special. Professional diplomat, remember?" He stroked her all over, his touch kindling flames of desire across her body.

She let all the joy and affection she felt for him fill her next words. "You are special. You are my true mate, Jet Tindor of Pyros. And I will be with you from now until we return to the flames that birthed us."

His breath caught. "Then I am a truly blessed male." He leaned back, coaxing her head up so they could gaze upon each other. "You are mine, Hanna Dewan. And you are all I will ever need."

She was his. Truly. Finally. His.

Desire burned through him, a bright white flame

that nothing but her could quench. He tore at her clothes, sending buttons flying and rending the delicate fabric of her blouse in his hurry to get her naked.

"Hey, I don't have that many outfits with me, and I already ruined one."

He nipped her lush lower lip as he swept a hand down her soft stomach and tore open the clasp of her slacks. "We'll go shopping later. Or I'll send my personal shopper out to get you some clothes."

She snickered. "You have a personal shopper?"

"Says the woman who has a personal assistant who probably knows your dress size, shoe size, list of favourite foods, and exactly how you like your coffee," he retorted.

"Huh. Guilty as charged. Only my assistant is now a dragon. I think that means I need to give her a raise."

She tugged his shirt over his head, nails grazing bare skin.

"You've got two dragons on the payroll, now. I'd suggest giving them both raises, and then installing fire extinguishers in all your offices. The first time one of you has a bad day, something is likely to catch fire."

"Good thinking." She grinned. "Speaking of fire…" She snapped her fingers and the two of them were suddenly engulfed in flames. Their clothes burned away in seconds, leaving her naked in his lap.

"Cheater."

"Just be glad your furniture is fireproof."

She was still laughing when he kissed her, their

tongues dancing, mouths mated. He opened the link between them and let her emotions wash over him. Need, affection, joy. He drank it all in until he was almost drunk with it.

"Bed now," she whispered.

"As my mate wishes."

He gathered her back into his arms and rose from the chair, carrying her to the bedroom with unabashed urgency. He wanted her too badly to go slowly. The Scorching might be ending, but his desire for Hanna would never fade.

He set her down in the middle of the bed and she stretched out with a languid sigh, arms over her head, hips raised in a sensual invitation.

He pounced onto the bed, catching her laughter in his mouth as he moved over her. Her legs parted, hips arching so her mons pressed against the throbbing shaft of his cock.

"Open the link between us. Feel me. Feel us." He wanted her to share this moment with him.

He knew the second she'd done it. Her beautiful eyes widened and her emotions grew stronger, amplified as they flowed back and forth between them. Arms braced on either side of her shoulders he held himself over her and she reached between them, soft fingers guiding his cock into position.

He pressed into her slowly, relishing the slick heat of her body as it welcomed him. "I love you."

She smiled up at him, her eyes bright and full of love. "*Tokee*," she whispered back in Pyrosian.

He threw back his head and laughed. "Yes, my love. I'm yours."

After that, they didn't need words. Their bodies came together and their souls danced, every thought, feeling, and desire shared. She writhed and moaned beneath him, every flex of her body and roll of her hips pushing him closer to the edge of his control.

He revelled in their intimacy, using it to give her everything she needed to reach her climax while basking in the truth of their bond. They were one now, and always would be.

That knowledge filled him with wild joy, and as he neared release, he let himself go. Hard thrusts, urgent kisses, he plunged into the whirlwind of their shared awareness and let it lift him into an orbit so high he could reach out to touch the stars.

When he came, it was with her name on his lips. Heart pounding, cock swelling to lock them together for a few last moments of intimacy, he leaned down and kissed her, breathing in her scent.

Her fingers stroked the back of his neck as contentment settled over him like a warm blanket. He held himself over her, looking down at his mate with wonder and gratitude. "I know you don't believe in them, but I will have to say a prayer of thanks to the Gods for bringing us together."

"I don't believe in them. Not yet. But I do believe

that *something* brought us together." She touched her chest, then his. "And if our bond isn't proof of magic, then I don't know what is."

"I don't care if you believe in my Gods, *tani*. So long as you always believe in us."

Hanna smiled, her eyes gleaming with tears he'd kiss away before they fell. "Always."

The End

ABOUT THE INTERGALACTIC DATING AGENCY SERIES

Ready for more out of this world romances? The adventure isn't over yet! Fly over to our dating agency website to check out more stories from this multi-author series. The Intergalactic Dating Agency is ready and waiting to set you up with a host of alien hotties from all over the galaxy.

Make a date with your alien match today.

http://romancingthealien.com

Want to read more stories with book boyfriends
that are out of this world?

**Check out Susan Hayes' other Science Fiction
Romance Titles**

<u>The Drift</u>
Double Down
All In
Wild Card
Three of a Kind
No Limit
Blind Bet
Aces Over Queen

<u>Nova Force</u>
Operation Phoenix
Operation Cobalt
Operation Fury

<u>3013: The Series</u>
3013: RENEGADE
3013: STOWAWAY
3013: TARGETED
3013: FATED
3013: SCARRED